The Book of the Sea

Also by Eric R. Asher

Keep track of Eric's new releases by receiving an email on release day. It's fast and easy to sign up for Eric's mailing list, and you'll also get an ebook copy of the subscriber exclusive anthology, *Whispers of War.*

Go here to get started: www.ericrasher.com

The Steamborn Trilogy:

Steamborn
Steamforged
Steamsworn

The Vesik Series:
(Recommended for Ages 17+)

Days Gone Bad
Wolves and the River of Stone
Winter's Demon
This Broken World
Destroyer Rising
Rattle the Bones
Witch Queen's War
Forgotten Ghosts
The Book of the Ghost
The Book of the Claw
The Book of the Sea
The Book of the Staff*
The Book of the Rune*

The Book of the Sails*
The Book of the Wing*
The Book of the Blade*
The Book of the Fang*
The Book of the Reaper*

The Vesik Series Box Sets

Box Set One (Books 1-3)
Box Set Two (Books 4-6)
Box Set Three (Books 7-8)
Box Set Four: The Books of the Dead Part 1
(Coming in 2020)*
Box Set Five: The Books of the Dead Part 2
(Coming in 2020)*

Mason Dixon – Monster Hunter:

Episode One
Episode Two
Episode Three

*Want to receive an email when one of Eric's books releases? Sign up for Eric's mailing list.
www.ericrasher.com

The Book of
the Sea

Eric R. Asher

Edited by Laura Matheson
Cover typography by Indie Solutions by Murphy Rae
Cover design ©Phatpuppyart.com – Claudia McKinney

~

Find the light in the darkness.

~

CHAPTER ONE

"ARE YOU NOT concerned your time may be better spent rallying the rest of your people?" Alexandra asked as she tightened the straps of Nixie's armor. "Damian is not our only priority."

Nixie flexed her hand and studied the back of the gauntlet she'd used to walk through the Abyss. "Every choice has a risk, Alexandra. This is no different."

"There are other weapons besides Damian that could win the war with Nudd." Alexandra tugged the last latch of the leg armor together at Nixie's thigh. "Pull your hair up."

Nixie did, carefully bundling it between her hands as she ignored Alexandra's prods. Of course, she knew there were other weapons, but the need to save Damian had more than one aspect. He was certainly a powerful weapon against Nudd, only a fool wouldn't be able to see that, but their love had become a symbol to her people, which meant Damian himself was now a symbol for everything she'd been trying to change among the water witches.

Alexandra patted Nixie's hand as the silver collar slid into place. "That is not to say you should abandon him."

"I know," Nixie said. "I couldn't do that even if it was the best decision for our people, but it's not. We need to pull him back from the brink."

Alexandra hesitated and held her tongue.

She didn't agree, and Nixie knew it. But Nudd had wronged her for the last time. No one, nothing, would stand in the way of their empire reborn. They would have peace and solidarity among the people, or they would have a war that could end in nothing but a pyrrhic victory.

An electronic buzz echoed through the old chamber. Though Nixie's initial reaction was to comment on how out of place the sound was, she knew it emanated from her phone.

Alexandra paused as she reached for the daggers on the table, instead opting for the small glowing screen of the phone. She frowned down at it and glanced back at Nixie. "It's Park."

"Put him on speaker," Nixie said. "I want you to hear whatever he has to say."

Alexandra slid her finger across the screen, and Park didn't wait for a greeting.

"Nixie? Is it true? You threatened members of the United Nations?"

Alexandra's eyebrow rose. Nixie had perhaps not told her the entire story of what had transpired in those chambers. No use glossing over it now.

"Yes. They're moving too slowly. Is that so different than what your own politicians do?"

Park groaned, his frustration echoing around the small war room. "Yes, it's a little bit different. When our idiot leaders threaten each other, it's expected. When a supernatural entity, one they didn't really believe existed until a year ago, threatens them, it's a *lot* different."

"Nudd has been a threat to them far longer than that."

"That's not the point," Park said. "You can't go around threatening world leaders and not expect some kind of reaction."

Nixie frowned in the general direction of the phone and muttered. "Perhaps I was mildly untoward. With Nudd's theft of the commoners' bombs, I can see why they'd be more sensitive." It sounded like more of an apology than she'd meant it to be. It was their very sensitivity to the fact those bombs had been stolen that Nixie had been counting on. They needed to be ready for a Fae attack, and if she was being honest with

3

herself, some of that attack might come from her own people. There were still witches loyal to Lewena, and would be until their dying day, when they joined the previous queen in oblivion.

"What's this thing Zola says you're after?" Park asked.

Alexandra leaned toward the phone. "Zola? I didn't realize Zola knew what we were after."

A puff of static echoed around them when Park sighed. "And who else is on this line?"

"Just me," Alexandra said, "and Nixie."

"Can one of you tell me what it is? An Eye of Atlantis?"

"Is this a question coming from you?" Nixie asked, "Or your superiors?"

Something squeaked and clicked in the background on the phone. "We're as secure here as we were in the underground base Aeros built for us."

Nixie sometimes wondered at the trust Damian and the others placed in the commoner. Military or not, he was still a commoner. But it was times like this she felt she could better understand. The security in the underground base hadn't been secure at all. They'd been infiltrated by Fae skilled in concealment and manipulation. The commoners would call it mind control, but it was different than that. It was a skill few beings possessed.

"It's not a weapon," Nixie said, and there was enough truth to that statement she felt it would hide the deception. But as with most tools of knowledge, a great many things could be used as weapons that were not meant to be.

"The Eye is only one core for the seal. It's one of the only chances we have to save them."

Even as the words left her mouth, she regretted the phrasing. She should've kept the focus on Damian. The military already knew about his loss. But they might not have known Sam and Vicky were tied to his fate. If Park caught her slip, he didn't mention it.

"How long will you be gone?" Park asked. "You're our strongest ally in Europe. You and the nation you lead. Is there a way we can reach you?"

Nixie looked to Alexandra. "You will not have a way of reaching me, but I will leave one of the Wasser-Münzen with Alexandra. She has authority among the undines. Reach out to her, should you have any need."

"My Queen—" Alexandra started in protest.

Nixie held up her hand. "I don't know how long I'll be gone, Park. If all goes well, it may be only a day or two. I know that can be an eternity at a time like this."

"And if it goes poorly?" Park asked.

Nixie grimaced. "Then it will no longer be a concern of mine. The crown will fall to another, and my people will be plunged back into chaos."

The silence told Nixie Park hadn't been expecting that response.

"Ask her," a voice whispered in the background. A voice Nixie thought she recognized.

More hushed muttering sounded over the line before Park said, "Okay, okay."

"What is it?" Nixie asked.

Park took a deep breath. "The Eye, is it in *Atlantis*? Is it a real place?"

"Was that Casper?" Nixie asked. She didn't like the idea of revealing too much about the fallen city of Atlantis. She hadn't been there in a long time, but the last time she'd laid eyes on it, only wildlife dwelled there. But Casper had old blood running through her veins. And like most Fae, Nixie favored the old families.

"It's me," Casper said, raising her voice before Park could respond. "I'm so sorry about Damian."

"It's okay." Nixie hesitated. "And thank you. As to your question, the Eye of Atlantis is believed to still be at the center of the old city. It's been at the bottom of the ocean for millennia. I haven't been there in almost half that time. I'm not sure what's left, if anything. The ocean can preserve wreckage at those depths, but there are other things that dwell in the deeps. Creatures that can swallow a city, or live within the fires of the deepest trenches."

"But you mean it's real?" Casper said. "Atlantis was a real place?"

Nixie exchanged a look with Alexandra.

"It always has been," Alexandra said. "There was a time commoners lived on the rings of the city, while the undines lived in the waters between each ring."

"Are you telling me you're heading to the ocean floor?" Park asked, his voice rising.

"Yes," Nixie said.

"You're going to need to tell me more about this if you survive," Park said.

"I will." Nixie looked at Alexandra and then turned her gaze to the phone. "The world knows about us once more. It's time the world learns more about the history it's forgotten."

"Good luck," Casper said. "We'll be thinking of you. Come back safe."

"Thank you," Nixie said. She nodded to Alexandra, and the other undine ended the call.

Alexandra picked the two gray daggers up from the shelf and walked toward her queen. Blades out, she slowly slid the deadly edge of each into their place at Nixie's side. One fit neatly into the empty sheath at

Nixie's waist. She kneeled for the other, sliding it into the armor that protected her queen's shin.

Nixie took a deep breath as Alexandra returned to the rack of weapons. The undine pulled one of the rarest weapons of the water witches from its home. A long slender blade, forged entirely of the gray metal of the stone daggers, whispered out of the rack where it had been stored for centuries. It was a sacred thing, and Alexandra handled it with the care due a fragile relic.

But Nixie had seen the swords of stone in battle before. There was nothing fragile about them. Unnatural durability, and the power to end the life of any water witch who crossed her path was an ability normally left to the queen and her guards. That was an unspoken law she'd already broken. She'd provided the commoners with the materials and the knowledge to strike down her own people. But if she hadn't, Lewena might have won. Nixie certainly wouldn't have been able to save Damian from the grasp of the old queen on the banks of the Missouri River, but Casper had. She'd taken Lewena down at a distance, with a bullet forged in the power of the stone daggers.

Nixie turned. Alexandra eased the sword's tip into the long scabbard hanging from the left side of Nixie's armor. Metal sang against metal until at last the silver cross-guard of the sword clicked against the scabbard's locket.

Alexandra walked around Nixie, checking the latches of her armor, an old ritual, one the pair had repeated for each other before many battles in the past millennia. Before she could complete her second circle, the armor sealed itself at the seams. The metal created a barrier between the silver plates that glowed briefly with electric blue energy. An enemy attempting to slide a dagger into a weak joint or hinge would be met with violent resistance.

Nixie took one last deep breath before she adjusted the crown upon her head. "I still don't like the idea of wearing this to Atlantis."

"If you encounter anyone from our domain, they won't see it as an aggression," Alexandra said. "I'm sure of it."

Nixie frowned. "I wish I had your confidence about that. We've left the city to the depths for centuries."

"Not so long when you live as long as we do." Alexandra clasped Nixie's shoulders. "Be careful, nonetheless. Nudd has unleashed things onto this world that should never have set foot upon it again."

Nixie closed her eyes and inclined her head. "That is why we war, my friend. When this war is done, may the days of killing die with it."

Nixie stepped away from Alexandra and ran her finger across the phone.

The line clicked to life before she had so much as a chance to rethink the choice.

A deep voice answered, a calming presence and an odd person to call friend. "You have Hugh."

Nixie smiled. "Wolf. I may be out of touch for a time."

"You've decided to return to Atlantis?"

"I have."

"Our first teacher is our own heart, friend. Travel safe."

"Spare me your proverbs. You know I wouldn't be doing this if it wasn't for Damian."

"Indeed," Hugh said.

Nixie blinked. "Damn it. Tell Haka not to put up with your nonsense for too long. That boy needs to get out from under your claws."

"You will survive this, old friend. If you fail, then Damian is truly lost. I don't believe you'll allow Sam and Vicky to die so easily."

Nixie's teeth slammed together. "Of course I won't," she snapped. "I was in that city when it fell. I know what Leviticus did, Hugh. The least I can do is help his student."

"The eldritch are returning," Hugh said. "Do not

forget that. If you need to wake the guardians, do not hesitate. It would not do the world well for you to be buried at sea."

She'd learned some of the old wolf's tricks. Even as the anger rose inside her, the realization of what he was doing calmed her.

"Thank you," Nixie said. "Thank you for the focus you've offered. I won't forget what you've said."

"It is not a time for calm," Hugh said. "This is the time of the storm, and you must meet it with fury."

"I will." She hesitated. "Do me a favor?"

"You need only ask."

"Take your own advice. You don't need to be the man behind the curtain."

"I am currently the man with the death bats," Hugh said, his voice fading slightly as he shifted on the other end of the line. "Zola has returned to the cabin. When you have the Eye, go to her. The Society of Flame has agreed to help track down the third core, but it will not be an easy journey."

"It never is. Take care of the pack."

"Tell Alexandra she breathes too loudly to be discreet."

Nixie grinned when she met the other undine's surprised gaze. The call ended, and Nixie let the screen fade to black.

Alexandra rubbed the back of her hand. "The eldritch beings are truly returning to the planes of the mortals?"

"Let us hope the worst of them stay locked in other realms, or frozen in the Abyss." Nixie's thoughts trailed to Damian. He was trapped there with those things, monsters out of time, out of sync with the realities they had yet to destroy. But in Damian's form, she suspected he wouldn't be at nearly as much risk as the creatures he might encounter, though there were stories of indestructible gods that roamed the place between worlds. She slid the Wasser-Münzen out of a leather pouch at her side and held it out to Alexandra.

"If you have need of me …" Alexandra started, but her words trailed off.

"If I do, I'll contact you. Have one of the fairies bring you as close as they can to Castillo San Felipe del Morro. From the watchtowers, the ruins are due north, into the trench."

"I know, my queen," Alexandra said with a weak smile. She reached out and wrapped her hand around Nixie's forearm.

Nixie returned the gesture, a symbol of both greeting and goodbye the wolves tended to use. It rankled the witches who still held some loyalty to the old rulers of the water witches. That in itself was enough to make

Nixie and her followers adopt it in earnest.

With their grip broken, Nixie headed to the silent waterfall at the other end of the chamber. Her skin grew translucent as she stepped inside, the chill water running through her veins as though it meant to freeze her in place. But that cold would be nothing compared to the freezing depths of the trench.

CHAPTER TWO

I T WASN'T NECESSARY for Nixie to step outside the Queen's Sanctuary to use the gauntlet, but somehow it felt right. She stared out at the sea crashing against the columns of Giant's Causeway.

Damian had unintentionally set her on a path to change the fate of her people. To give them a better life, a more fulfilling time as they lived through the ages. The least she could do was try to save Sam and Vicky. It's what he'd want. Somewhere, in the darkest part of her heart, she knew the chance of even Gaia being able to save Damian was merely a spark in a crushing darkness.

But Nixie knew darkness. And she knew what to do with it. Fire could light the shadows, and rage could burn them down. There was a time for mercy, but this was not it.

Nixie struck the back of her gauntlet and ripped two fingers down it. The light left the world, and blackness rose to greet her.

✦ ✦ ✦

NIXIE STRODE FORWARD before the light resolved around her. The golden path, so dim as to be only an afterimage at first, solidified beneath her feet. Gaia wasn't here, but she didn't need to be. It gave Nixie a small comfort knowing the titan was keeping watch over Damian. If anything too untoward moved on him, Gaia could hopefully keep Damian far away.

But the fact Gaia wasn't there meant Nixie's senses were straining at every whisper around her. The Abyss, infinite in its darkness, was not a silent place. A thunder like the groan of a giant rumbled around her. As she cocked her head to listen, the gauntlet produced a tug on her being that was familiar now, and she kept to the left at the first intersection she encountered.

It was there, in the golden glow beneath the road, she saw the churning mass of what could have been mistaken for thunderclouds. If clouds were covered in a thousand eyes and the gaping maw of the damned. Teeth like needles flexed, layering together until they seemed a mesh screen, only to expand and blossom once more, revealing the rotten black and green flesh within.

There were few sights that unsettled Nixie. She'd seen more than one apocalypse befall her own people, and that didn't touch on the atrocities she'd seen the commoners endure. But this undulating mass, the slow swivel of a thousand blood red eyes focusing on her, caused Nixie to step away from the edge of the golden path. Her steps accelerated, carrying her away from that nightmare ever faster.

Nixie frowned when the path dove into a steep descent. Every step felt as though she could lose her balance and slide off into the darkness. For there were no rails in that place, no place to catch yourself if you fell into the pit. She wondered if there would be another path below, or if falling from the path was a death sentence. But that's where Damian was now, wasn't it? She shook her head to clear the thought.

The golden glow beneath her feet leveled off at another fork in the road, but now there were three paths. Times like this, she wished she had Gaia's ability to walk a more direct line to her destination. Every time she entered the Abyss, the path was unpredictable, ever-changing, though it did not normally split so often. Perhaps it made some kind of sense because her destination was different each time, but it felt wrong.

Nixie closed her eyes and held the gauntlet to her chest, but there was not a single pull waiting to show her the way. There were two.

"Are you fucking kidding me?" Nixie said, her eyes flashing open as she scowled at the gauntlet. Once again, the familiar throb pulled her forward, toward the middle path, but a second pull coaxed her toward the right. "Shit."

"It's Damian, isn't it?" she whispered to the gauntlet. "I confused you somehow." Nixie closed her eyes and took a deep breath, focusing all her energy and intent on Atlantis. That's where she needed to go, but the gauntlet didn't respond.

Nixie growled at the metal wrapped around her hand. She steadied herself again, this time remembering the walls of the fort on the corner of what the commoners called San Juan.

The thought triggered a memory she'd nearly forgotten.

✦   ✦   ✦

SHE STOOD UPON the walls of that place with Euphemia soon after the commoners had built it. A pirate they'd met had told them about the legend of Atlantis. It had been such an entertaining, if somewhat inaccurate, tale that the undines had let him live to find the rum he'd been so desperately seeking for his wife.

But what the pirate hadn't known was that he'd been standing on the fragmented shores of what had once been the great continent of Atlantis. And deep beneath his feet waited the ruins of the old city. That's where she needed to be now, to save Damian, to preserve the empire of the water witches.

✦   ✦   ✦

NIXIE GASPED WHEN the tug from the gauntlet almost knocked her over. It was the middle path, of that there was no doubt. Her eyes flew open, and she screamed.

Marching before her was an army of stone undines. Lewena led them all. While they appeared to be still at first, a shimmer of light like an oil spill washed over them, and the bodies moved. Caught in their death poses as if finely carved marble, the faces twisted and contorted, weapons rising as the odd shimmer bled across them.

Nixie looked down at the gauntlet, and it spoke once more. The way to Atlantis was through them, through that field of damned souls trapped for all time. She ground her teeth and drew the stone sword from its scabbard.

Mercy had no place here.

Lewena screeched as Nixie's blade shattered her body into its component pieces. Witch after witch fell until she slowly realized every face she knew, every body one she had fought or loved or slayed. Faces she'd nearly forgotten from the past. Opposing soldiers who only lived in her memory as victories. They were all here, all taunting her, all digging their rough flesh into her psyche.

The farther she crashed through the line of living statues, the deeper a path she carved into her own memories until finally *he* was there, chin raised to the black heavens, and the crown upon his head. The last king of the undines. The man she'd helped throw down into oblivion and establish the matriarchy that would reign for over six millennia.

But he'd been a father, a husband to the first queen, and though it was the queen who betrayed him to his death, the vision of the child beside him tried to tear Nixie's heart from her chest. She raised the stone sword and screamed.

"I'm sorry!"

The sword crashed down onto the old king's crown, shattering it as surely as his body crumbled around her. With that there was a path, a way through, and the gauntlet tugged on her once more. Nixie's guilt washed away in a rage as she realized something was toying with her, pulling memories from her mind to obstruct her path through the Abyss.

She focused on every step and let the anger well up as she sprinted past the last of the echoes of the past. They would always be a part of her legacy, but the world was different now. There was more to this world than surviving, more than killing. But if she had to, she'd kill to protect the ones she loved. Channeling that rage would be the easiest thing in the world.

The gray bodies vanished and the gauntlet pulsed around Nixie's hand. She wiped the tears from her cheek with a violent swipe of her fingers and let the gauntlet rip her out of the Abyss.

CHAPTER THREE

DARKNESS GAVE WAY to light, and the blue skies of the Caribbean threatened to blind her with their fury. Nixie blinked in the brightness, raising her hand to shield her eyes. She winced when the sunlight reflected off her armor and hit her eyes again anyway.

"Cool costume!"

Nixie turned to find a young girl looking up at her. "It's not … thank you."

"Did you see her, Mom?" the girl asked, skipping away and tugging on an older woman's arm. "Is that how the guards used to dress here?"

"I … don't think so," the mother said, lifting a skeptical eyebrow. "I really don't think so."

Nixie looked around at the old gray and beige weatherworn stone beneath her feet. Cannons lined the wall between ramparts. The breeze picked up and she caught the scent of the fishing boats in the bay mixed with the salt of the ocean. A watchtower jutted out over the sea from a narrow path. Nixie hurried down that path, her armor scraping against stone so dark it was almost black. From the narrow windows, she could clearly see the ocean and the structure of the western walls of the fort around her.

The gauntlet hadn't led her wrong. This was El Morro. She was in Puerto Rico, one of the surviving fragments of the continent of Atlantis. That meant the ruins of the city rings were due north, deep in an oceanic trench.

Small waves boiled along the shoals on the shore below, a low rocky barrier that would have protected this place from erosion and invaders alike in the past. And the fort had done its job in that, repelling more than one navy with their sights set on the island.

Shouts of alarm drew Nixie's attention. She turned away from the seas and hurried deeper into the fort, climbing stairs through a dim tunnel that flanked either side of a rough ramp. The sky opened again, revealing bright goldenrod walls and graceful white arches. Nixie sprinted through an archway and up another, gentler slope, crossing back onto the exterior of the fort until she came to a watchtower jutting out from the wall.

Beyond the outer wall of the fort waited a sweeping vista of neatly manicured grass populated by dozens of families flying kites in front of Old San Juan. But another scream rose up, and her gaze snapped to the south. Her stomach churned and her knuckles whitened between the joints of the gauntlet.

There, deeper in the bay, a shadow rose.

"Gods no," Nixie whispered. "Nudd, you bastard."

A slender fin crested the water near a cruise ship, and at the other end of the ship, tentacles as thick as dolphins erupted from the water. They snapped out, tearing away lifeboats and railings as if they were paper.

Nixie ran flat out. She needed to get to the ocean, and *now*. Commoners knew what giant squids were, but this … this was something different. It didn't need the depths of the trenches to survive. It was a different kind of monster altogether, more like the leviathans. She hurdled a wall and dropped to a lower ramp, sprinting toward water. Her boots scraped and clanged against the massive stones of the shoreline, and then she dove.

Warm water embraced her, and Nixie shot through it like a bullet. She couldn't battle a leviathan like that alone, but those people were going to die by the hundreds if she did nothing. The only chance she had, *they* had, was a guardian out of legend. A beast the likes of which the commoners had never seen. But was it still alive? And would it still heed the order of a queen? She'd have her answer soon enough.

Nixie passed out of the bay, circling around the old fort until she reached the saltier waters of the ocean, and then dove straight down. It didn't take long for her to find the ocean bottom, skimming along the mud and silt and rather surprised fish. She was close to the edge of the trench that would lead her to the ruins of Atlantis, but those pits weren't her goal this time.

Instead, she closed her eyes, held her hand over her heart, and spoke an incantation that had not been heard in millennia.

"Omnes Orbis Periculum!"

The world shook.

✦　　✦　　✦

THE SHELLS AND sand and mud of the ocean floor shifted. Nixie felt the wave as a titanic slab of earth rose. If she wasn't careful, the force would escape, rush to the northwest where it could scour islands on its journey to drown the Florida coast.

But she felt the surge of line energy that poured through her crown with a fury, concentrated, amplified, until she could direct the force of the ocean skyward. Amber eyes rose from that cascade of mud and death. A guardian who had not woken since Atlantis sank. A beast the commoners thought of as nothing but a relic from the time of dinosaurs.

The massive jaws flexed, revealing hundreds of deadly triangular teeth and a long scaly head as its body shook off its lengthy sleep.

"Leviathans have attacked. Guard this place."

Mud swirled around the beast, and though its reptilian head, not so different than a crocodile, dwarfed Nixie, it waited for her to swim up and settle in at the base of its skull. She gripped a ridge that tapered off behind one of the nearly person-sized eyes. The giant gave one violent swipe of its tail followed by a broad stroke of its flippers. They surged forward, leaving a tower of mud and debris to settle once more to the ocean floor.

This was one of the guardians of Atlantis. A creature the humans had come to call a Mosasaurus, but they couldn't have imagined the power and magic that kept the immortal guardians alive through the ages. Those they'd discovered in the fossil record had been children of giants, rivals to the titans of old.

The return to the bay was swift, and Nixie couldn't deny the thrill that lanced through her stomach riding the legendary creature. This was right. This was good. The leviathan wouldn't stand a chance. She leaned in against the small smooth scales of the beast's neck.

"Do you see it?"

They rose higher in the water until both Nixie and the guardian's tail would occasionally break the surface of the waves. The guardian growled beneath her, a vibration that sent ripples to her core.

The giant squid came into focus, fragments of the cruise ship splashing down around them, some sinking to the floor of the bay while others remained floating. More than one of the beast's arms snapped inward to where its beak would be. Nixie's exhilaration soured at the thought of what the thing might be eating.

"Spare the ship. Kill the leviathan!"

The mantle of the squid breached the surface of the water as it hoisted itself higher with three of its eight arms. The guardian stayed near the top of the ocean now, angling for the leviathan like a torpedo.

But the eldritch things hadn't destroyed worlds and survived the Abyss by being blind to their environment. The Mosasaurus opened its jaws and gave a violent snap of its tail. But one of the squid's tentacles lashed out, carving a path along the guardian's head and nearly taking Nixie's hand with it.

Nixie drew her sword out of instinct, landing an awkward blow against the thick appendage, scarcely giving it more than a paper cut. But the Mosasaurus sensed its prey. It gave a savage twist of its head and locked down on the leviathan's tentacle.

They broke the surface of the water as the beast tore at the tentacle. The entire ship listed as the guardian dragged the squid and the hull closer to shore. The guardian released a booming growl before its jaws opened and it lunged, latching onto the siphon below the squid's massive eye.

Ink blasted out across the guardian's snout, but the Mosasaurus held fast. It shook its head violently enough to dislodge Nixie. She summoned the waters to rise before her, directing a stream to wash away as much of the ink from the guardian's eyes as she could.

The squid's tentacles tore deeper into the ship, and the shouts from above grew more frantic. Nixie looked up and saw the family. A young mother with a chair in one hand and the other holding back her son. She bashed at the tentacle, bellowing at the beast attacking her family. The squid searched blindly, but it would only be moments before it found them, or the guardian's attack dumped them out of their room.

Even as Nixie thought it, the Mosasaurus started a death roll. Its jaws locked into the squid, the guardian spun. The ship tilted, and the family screamed as they fell.

Line energy spiked through Nixie's armor, lighting her crown like an electric blue beacon, and the ocean responded like she'd never felt before. She'd meant to raise the water to greet the falling family. Instead, the bay itself rose to push against the ship, steadying the vessel as the family splashed down, and the arms of the squid broke away to the gory sound of snapping flesh and cables that could not bear the weight.

The severed appendages writhed on the lower deck while another appendage, that had been attached to a smoke stack, spasmed and fell away. Nixie swooped beneath it, gathering up the family in the ocean and raising them back onto a higher deck with a torrent of water.

She didn't pause as the mother shouted her thanks. Nixie used the momentum of the water to rocket through a shattered bank of windows on the bridge.

"Who the fuck are you!"

Nixie turned toward the voice and found the disheveled captain pointing a flare gun at her. She raised her hands anyway.

"Nixie of Atlantis, Queen of the Undines, here to save your ship. Unless you'd prefer to shoot me?"

The man's eyes hadn't gotten any wider, so Nixie was pretty sure he was in shock.

"Can you steer?"

The captain shook his head. "That … that thing damaged the propellers."

Nixie glanced out the window behind her. The

ocean boiled, blood and ink churning up as the guardian spun. Whirlpools of gore and ink spread out around the beast.

"It's dead now. Let's get you to shore."

The captain hesitated.

Nixie gave him a small smile. "I'll push. You steer. Be ready."

"What?"

But with that she was out the window, and the water rushed up to greet her. The water might have been brackish before, but now it was downright muck. The fight between the leviathan and the guardian had stirred up mud and debris, and that didn't count the sheer quantity of blood all around.

Nixie reached the mangled metal that had been a propeller blade, but the rudders were still intact. The hull was dented, and the captain was lucky his ship hadn't been sunk. If they'd been any later ... She shook her head. Nixie opened her palm and the waters responded.

This wasn't the overpowering surge she'd felt when she'd been in a panic to save that family. This was a constant pressure, a gentle prodding, that slowly pushed the ship forward.

It wasn't far to the docks, and for that she was thankful. Whatever additional strength the crown gave her, there was still a limit, and the fatigue was real by the time they reached the docks at San Juan a few minutes later.

Once the ship had settled, she waved to the captain. She didn't see the family again, but she wasn't surprised. Who in their right mind would want to be anywhere close to the railings after that? A few people, apparently, as they poked their heads out, but not many.

Nixie turned to the guardian. He'd finished his dinner, and now floated calmly in the bay like the world's biggest murder log. Nixie smiled to herself when she remembered Damian's name for alligators, but it was quickly replaced by a heaviness in her chest.

She had another mission, and that meant it was time to go home.

CHAPTER FOUR

NIXIE SWAM BESIDE the guardian as they left the bay, angling toward the Mosasaurus's resting place. She thought about leaving the guardian there to settle into the mud and debris above the chasm, but the thought of what might wait below chased the idea away.

Instead, they dove together. The guardian's tail snapped and rocketed the beast forward, cutting through the water fast enough that Nixie had to pull on the ley lines to match the guardian's speed.

The relative brightness of the shallows dimmed, and the warmth of the waters turned to a bitter chill. Undines were built for the seas and, without thinking, Nixie's body changed. The magic flowing through her veins shifted, adapting to the cold until she didn't feel it anymore. Her vision dimmed as her eyes altered in the depths, and the shadows of the trench resolved into fractured stone and a brilliant array of anemones.

The color of those creatures, and the gray of nearby

sharks, faded, replaced by clouds of debris and tiny clusters of swimming creatures surrounding Nixie and the guardian. Their speed and wake dislodged a small avalanche of silt and stone that clouded the ocean above them.

In moments, they passed out of the zone most commoners were familiar with. They hadn't managed to reach the floor of the trench yet, but Nixie suspected it was only a matter of time. Bright fish and flora were replaced by an odd glow. Intermittent glimpses of distended mouths and hanging lures in front of needle-like teeth showed Nixie an array of anglerfish. Though they were terrifying at first glance, Nixie had spent more than one day in the depths, watching the creatures hunt.

The bioluminescence of the anglerfish faded, and the glow around Nixie's armor brightened, giving off just enough light for her altered eyes to pick out the walls of the trench, and any threats waiting nearby.

But what she saw wasn't a threat. It was a squat little octopus the commoners had taken to calling Dumbo. Stubby arms gracefully pulsed as its body compressed and its oversized "ears" slid through the water. As fast as it had arrived, the creature vanished into the shadows.

Sea stars with long frilled arms crawled past on the

sand and stone, searching out their next meal. But their slow-moving bodies returned to the darkness as quickly as they'd come into her vision.

An eel slithered past, darting into a crack in the jagged rocks near a small sponge as the looming shadow of the Mosasaurus crossed its path. Deeper, even sponges became sparse, and on the shelves of rock where carcasses had fallen, Nixie could see small clusters of snailfish swarming the remains.

They were far beyond where humans could survive now, and what waited below meant death and oblivion to most life of the world.

But they weren't alone. Giant anglerfish, far larger than Nixie had ever seen prowled the deeps. She couldn't imagine what the monstrous fish had been feeding on until something white and armored scuttled past and wedged itself into a narrow crevasse.

Things had changed in the depths of the trench.

Before she could register what had happened, another of the squid-like leviathans surged out of a cavern. The jaws of the guardian snapped closed around it in a heartbeat, severing the tip of the mantle and leaving a trail of tentacles to drift toward the sea floor where they stirred the mud and sand. Tentacles and debris vanished as the guardian gulped down its snack and they continued on.

The Mosasaurus slowed, circling the bottom of the trench while Nixie floated in the depths, eyeing the lights waiting beyond the collapsed ribs of the ancient city. What had been a canal when Atlantis ruled the Atlantic had fractured and fallen, only to sink into the muddy banks and provide a different path than the one that had once been for boats and triremes.

She held a hand up to the guardian. "Go. I will return."

The creature circled her twice with slow sweeps of its tail before drifting up into darkness. Nixie's gaze trailed away from the retreating guardian and focused on the tunnel before her.

It didn't appear much had changed since the last time Nixie had visited Atlantis. Centuries might have passed, but the entryway remained untouched. She drifted to the bottom until her boots made contact with the mud. Even in her current form, she started to sink into the debris. Nixie grimaced and pulled herself free, deciding to float just above the surface instead of risking getting her boots stuck.

The light from her armor showed enough detail she could see that the archway she now floated through had once belonged to the outer wall of Atlantis. Discolored brass lined the stone, and Nixie remembered what it was like when it had been above the sea and polished: a shining beacon to all who would visit, a second sun on the horizon for any ship sailing into its sights.

But that was no more. Now it was broken, lost forever in darkness, except for the sparse lights in the distance drifting in the cavern of the city.

Nixie needed the Eye of Atlantis, and she knew it would be near the center of the fallen city. When last she'd visited, she'd found fragments of the Temple of Poseidon: pinnacles coated in gold and mangled pillars with a silver sheen. The undines hoarded their treasure in the temple, and more than one map had been found in the room she'd inherited as queen. When the city sank, it didn't come down in one piece. It fractured and shifted, striking the ocean bottom in various areas before the continent itself collapsed around it. An insurmountable mountain of earth buried much of the city, but other parts remained trapped in hollows and caverns. Supports rigid enough to stand up to the crushing depths of the ocean held the stone above it.

Nixie passed the edge of the discolored brass walls and the narrow tunnel expanded into the first cavern. Here a guard tower stood, almost as if it had been designed to always be there. But it sat at a slight angle, and the architects of Atlantis would never have allowed such a departure from perfection.

Another light bloomed deeper in the cavern. And then another. When she'd seen them from a distance, she'd assumed they were deep sea anglerfish, perhaps not as massive as the mutations she'd found earlier, but durable enough to survive at this depth.

But the lights didn't move. They didn't dance in front of a menacing mouth of teeth. Nixie's pace slowed. Instead of continuing forward, she drifted toward an overturned aqueduct. It gave her shelter and concealed her movements as she ducked inside the upturned trough, shooting forward deeper into the cavern. It didn't much matter what the things were. They were between her and the Eye, between her and what she needed to help Damian. That meant she'd either pass by them unnoticed, or slaughter them on the spot.

Halfway through the aqueduct, Nixie dimmed her armor. The intricate silver no longer cast an eerie electric blue glow around her. Now there was only darkness, except for the lights that still shone in the cavern.

Nixie reached the edge of the aqueduct and stayed close to the ocean floor. Her boot brushed what should have been mud and silt. She frowned when the metal thumped against stone. The sediment had been scoured away by something. Perhaps the aqueduct had become home to a creature, but whatever the cause, she figured it would be best to move away from it.

She slipped out and took shelter behind an ornate pillar from a fallen temple. Nixie glanced up at the dented statue standing beside it. It was one of the original ten kings of Atlantis, a statue that had once stood in the outer ring of the city and marked a zone of private dwellings there. Nixie drifted up toward the top of the pillar until she reached the peak of the shattered support and slid onto the rough stone.

She was closer to the lights now, but she could only see two of them hovering between the squat stone buildings that once housed merchants and families. Before there had been at least ten of the lights, and Nixie frowned at the change.

"Move and you die," a smooth deep voice said behind her.

Nixie didn't speak. She moved. Magic channeled through her armor and she rocketed forward, far faster than whoever had spoken could keep up. In one move, she drew the sword from her belt and turned it on the man who had dared threaten her. But as she twisted toward him, her blade stopped cold. A face she had not seen in a millennium greeted her.

"Pace?" The name trailed off and echoed in the water of the cavern.

"Stand down!" he shouted, the deep blue of his skin a natural camouflage in the shadowy cavern. Only as he said the words did Nixie realize there was another of the blue men behind her. They'd always been stealthy hunters, a force to be reckoned with, and a rival to the undines in the deadliness of their skills.

"What are you doing here?" Nixie asked.

"Rebuilding what we lost. We spent centuries around Scotland, taking what and who we wanted. But that kind of piracy …" He patted his chest and lowered his trident. "It leaves a hole. We needed a home."

Nixie eyed the man. "I understand."

Pace frowned at her, the bluish flesh of his forehead furrowing. Midway down his waist, his body turned into more of a fish than a man. But the entirety of him was blue, which is where the blue men of the Minch had gotten their name.

"You wear the queen's crown." His tail swished and he locked his gaze on her. "What has happened?"

"A great deal of things," Nixie said. "A very great deal."

More lights flashed on around them until, after a time, the entire cavern lit up like a city at night.

Pace gestured to Nixie. "Come. Tell us why you're here. Tell us why you've returned after all this time. I thought the undines had left this place forever after it fell. We've seen a few of you return over the years, though we normally watch from the shadows. Our people have not always been allies."

Nixie gave him an empty smile. "You've always had a gift for understatement."

"And you have always had a gift for dismemberment."

Nixie's smile turned sly. She'd play his game for now, but if he stood in her way, she'd remind him exactly why she had that reputation.

CHAPTER FIVE

"IT'S BEEN NEARLY a century since we've seen any outsiders here," Pace said.

Nixie almost argued at being called an outsider, but even though she'd once called Atlantis home, this was no longer what that great city had been. Instead, she nodded and studied the dwellings Pace and his people had rebuilt.

"I remember that courtyard," Nixie said, gesturing to a fractured marble statue that had once been a fountain above the seas. She drifted closer to it and swiped away a thin layer of sediment around the base.

"Seeing if we pillaged the orichalcum?"

Nixie glanced up at the blue man. "I wasn't, but I was curious if it was still here. You know, more than one story laid the blame for the sinking of Atlantis at the feet of our greed."

Pace nodded. "Of course, had that been true, you wouldn't find a scrap of metal left down here."

Nixie rubbed her fingers together, feeling the

smooth silt sliding between them. "I imagine there wouldn't be. You know most of the commoners don't believe orichalcum ever existed?"

Pace shook his head. "Ridiculous. It was an attractive alloy, nothing more."

"Perhaps a bit more." Nixie looked toward a small tunnel as a row of lights appeared inside of it. She frowned at the dim shadows.

"Would you like to see the rest of the city?" As if Pace's question had been a signal, their escort of blue men drifted away. A few headed for the tunnel, while others vanished into the rebuilt dwellings and guard houses.

"There's more?" Nixie asked. "The Temple of Poseidon?"

Pace narrowed his eyes a fraction. "You are not here for the deserters, are you?"

"Deserters?" Nixie frowned.

"Come," Pace said after a moment's consideration, gesturing for Nixie to follow. "There are others who may like to meet you."

Before they reached the tunnel, Pace's hand flashed out and grabbed Nixie's arm. "Be still. We are not alone."

Nixie followed his gaze and the irritation at his touch faded. One of the massive anglerfish drifted by overhead, its lure a beacon in the shadows.

"What the hell happened to those things?"

Pace glanced at her and slowly released his grip on her arm. "Some fifty years ago the commoners started using the trench as a disposal site. They dropped barrels of drugs, some called steroids, others we could not pronounce."

He nodded to the giant above them. "Some of the wildlife consumed the waste. The mutation was rapid. Only a few generations before their size grew to be a threat."

"Why do you not slay them?" Nixie asked.

Pace gave a humorless laugh. "They are not harmful to us so long as we are careful to avoid them. And can you imagine a more frightening deterrent should the commoners reach these depths one day?"

Nixie cocked an eyebrow. "You're using them as guard dogs."

Pace grinned in earnest. "An apt description."

The jaws floated past, teeth as long as Nixie's forearms protruding from the gruesome face.

"Beware the lights, my queen, for they are most often not your friend." With that, Pace led the way into the lighted tunnel, his body gliding in an effortless arc with broad strokes of his tailfin.

Pace was disarming. That wasn't a trait Nixie remembered of the blue men of the Minch. Blood and savagery, those were her most vivid memories of Pace's people. They had a history to rival Graybeard's when it came to plunder and piracy. Only whereas Graybeard might have spared the lives of many commoners, the blue men didn't.

Nixie's hand drifted down to hover near the hilt of a stone dagger. She didn't need to get caught off guard any more than she already had been.

They passed the lights, and Nixie marveled at the lanterns housing the golden flames. Pulsing orbs brightened and dimmed inside ancient orichalcum vessels. The golden alloy had retained much of its color in the depths of the sea.

It was about that time Nixie recognized some of the metalwork inlaid along the ceiling of the tunnel. It had once been part of a beautiful mosaic that lined the bottom of one of the watery rings of Atlantis. This was a place where her people used to live, and the commoners would sail their ships above. But now it was broken, fallen to the bottom of the ocean, where it had been inverted and changed and lost.

Seeing that place pulled at the hollowness in her chest. It carved a wound in her defenses, so that instead of being on high alert for anything looking to ambush them, she was instead remembering the past. Remembering a life that had long been gone.

"Tell me about the deserters," Nixie said, making an effort to keep her voice steady. She hoped the change in conversation would bring the focus back to her attention. The blue men would know how to kill an undine. Of course, she knew well how to kill a blue man, too.

Pace didn't answer.

"I'm not here for them."

"I am glad of that," Pace said. "But you must understand, the deserters came here with their own story. One that I found somewhat hard to believe. They say another undine is looking to overthrow the queen. And last I had heard, Lewena was the queen of the water witches. So perhaps their concerns are not so unfounded?"

This was what Nixie had been worried about. She could lie to them, but he might be testing her. She figured that only gave her one real option. "The world above the sea has changed. And you need to know what's going on."

Pace released a humorless laugh. "My Queen, we are in one of the deepest trenches of this world. This is one of the few places we do not need to be concerned about the commoners."

"And yet they've poisoned your water. Mutated the

wildlife here. You said yourself those anglerfish were the commoners' doing."

Pace didn't respond.

"Gwynn Ap Nudd has torn Falias out of Faerie. Killed millions of commoners in the process. Started a war only he wanted. But the commoners can be as stubborn as he is. Warmongers alike, for that they surely have in common."

Pace slowed. "No king would do that."

"Agreed," Nixie said. "But not only did the king do that, but Lewena, then queen of the water witches, joined him. Together with Hern, they set out to rain destruction on both their enemies in Falias, and the commoners."

"I never much liked Hern," Pace said. "A pompous fool, so tied up in the old ways he would give his life to see them preserved."

Nixie shrugged. "And perhaps he did. For Nudd had other goals. Damian, the necromancer known as the mortal prince of the water witches, was one of Nudd's targets. He trapped them both, awoke a force in Damian ..." Nixie's words trailed off. She wasn't sure how to say it, and she didn't want to say it.

"Like Leviticus?" Pace asked, an edge to his voice.

Nixie couldn't remember if the blue men had been at the fall of Atlantis. There were details she found difficult to recall about the end of that era. But one that always remained vivid was the colossal form of Levi trying to save the city. Nixie shook her head. "Like him, but not like him. This is darker. Nudd's playing with forces he doesn't understand. And I suppose that makes a kind of sense, because Nudd is the Mad King."

Pace froze before continuing on. "So that's what happened to him." He rubbed slowly at his jaw. "That surprises me less than other things you've told me here. But it confirms what some of the deserters have said. And they tell me that if an undine comes here who is not a servant of Lewena, they will be hunting them."

"I am servant to none, and I hunt no one."

Pace cast a glance over his shoulder. "Then tell me, Queen, why are you here?" He enunciated each syllable, betraying the fact that his patience was wearing to some degree. Nixie wasn't sure how far she could push him, so she needed to figure out where the Eye of Atlantis was before things went bad.

A small stone basket caught Nixie's eye. It was broken, cracked into three pieces, and much of the detail had been worn away from the stone. But that wear hadn't come from the fall. This was a place of offering, one of the many places visitors and residents of Atlantis would leave ten portions of an offering.

"Well?" Pace asked.

"I'm not here for the deserters," Nixie said. "I am glad to hear of their survival, but I just need the Eye of Atlantis. It may be the only way to spare us all in this war."

"The Eye?" Pace said. "That is not what I expected you to be here for. I suppose it makes some sense now, how you were asking about the Temple of Poseidon." He nodded.

"Can you take me there?"

"Of course," Pace said. "But the Eye of Atlantis is not mine to give."

Nixie studied the blue man for a moment, waiting for him to explain. But as the silence grew longer, she realized he wasn't going to without prompting. She watched the tunnel behind her, and saw no sign of ambush, so decided to play his game.

"Then whose place is it?" Nixie asked. "If not the queen of the water witches, the ruler over those who first placed the Eye in this great city, then who?"

Pace narrowed his eyes and stared at Nixie. "And what would you do if we acquiesced? Millennia of rage and hatred are condensed into that artifact. It fuels the undines here, grants them the ability to survive in the shadows."

"Inspires them, perhaps," Nixie said. "Gives them hope you might say? But it does not grant them their ability to survive here. I once believed it was only possible to rule with an iron fist. With a sharp sword held to your enemy's throat. But what I didn't understand was that those we saw as enemies were not always against us."

"A foolish thought," Pace said. "Trust and loyalty will earn you a knife in the back. Blind trust will earn you many more."

Nixie slowly shook her head and let her hand fall away from the hilt at her waist. "You misunderstand. And I say again, the world above has changed. The Fae war among themselves."

"Bah!" Pace snapped. "That is no change at all."

Nixie offered him a patient smile. "What I've told you has already come to pass. I've taken the crown of the undines. And my mate is a necromancer, a mortal."

"I have no love lost for the water witches," Pace said. "But to think you would sully your own courts, your own throne, with a mortal mate. It is disgusting." He turned away again. "Regardless, I think it's time you met the deserters."

Nixie didn't rise to his bait. Instead, she returned her attention to the ruins around them.

The city of Atlantis had been miles across. How much of it had survived the fall was a mystery to Nixie. She thought only the fragments of the temple she'd seen in the past were all that remained of the great Temple of Poseidon. Pace had indicated otherwise. But how deep was it buried? How many more tunnels would they have to travel through? Nixie knew each tunnel they passed through lessened her chance of escape and gave the advantage to those who knew this place.

Before she finished the thought, they exited the other side of the old canal. What had been brass on the walls shifted to tin. It should have been a greater distance from the outer ring. Clearly, when the city had fallen and fractured, the layout had become something unrecognizable. If not for the silvery metal covering the walls, Nixie wouldn't have been able to identify the center regions of Atlantis.

"The place has changed quite a bit," Pace said.

Nixie paused before a collapsed pile of what had once been the sections of an ionic column. She'd seen its like many times before, but most of the temples to Hephaestus lay in a similar state of ruin. No gleaming metal adorned these columns. Because, to the water witches, Hephaestus had been a demon. An enemy like no other, but the demon those legends had been based on was now someone Nixie called a friend. And it was an odd thing, how time could change some things.

More lights came on around them, and Nixie could

see that the chamber they were in now was far larger than the first. This was a cavern of monumental proportions.

"So many of the buildings survived," Nixie said. "I'm surprised to see it." Even as she said this, she studied the surviving temples, the schools, and even some of the old bath houses still standing, and what had once been the central ring of the city.

Atlantis had always had more of the ionic architecture than any other style. But in the bath houses she could make out the intricate tops of Corinthian pillars, and beyond those a few Doric columns remained, crowned with sweeping scroll-like carvings.

"Not all of it had survived as well as you see today," Pace said. "My people rebuilt some of it, and deserters helped rebuild a great deal of the rest. Regardless, it was surprising how much of the old city remained intact. I can't say if someone had been here before us, but if they had been, they didn't stay."

Nixie nodded. She had been there herself, though she'd never dreamed so much of the ruin could have been restored. She'd pulled statues from the fallen city, victims of the battle at the end of Atlantis. Friends, and even some she thought of as family. So many didn't survive.

When she remembered those days, the fires that

tore through the city, the magic that poisoned them all, she could understand Lewena a little bit better. No matter how much time had passed, memories of the fall of Atlantis left a bitter taste in her mouth and a darkness in her heart.

Another series of lights joined them in the darkness and Pace started toward them. These were not the floating white orbs of an incantation, but the golden light of one of the fixed lanterns. Only there were dozens leading up a step-like structure, and a moment later Nixie realized she was looking at a section of the old stadium.

It was a strange sight, seeing it broken off as it was, half of it embedded in the wall, and the rest lost. But it created something like an auditorium, and in the stands waited a few dozen water witches.

"Those are the deserters," Pace said, apparently bent on stating the obvious, perhaps in a failed effort to hide his anger. "Let them decide your fate. I have no interest in the Eye."

Nixie glanced at him. Shouts rose as they reached the platform before the stands. And she had little doubt this wasn't going to go well.

CHAPTER SIX

"**Y**OUR ATTENTION, PLEASE," Pace said, raising a hand.

But the undines didn't respond to the blue man. They grew louder, several floating above the stands and screaming down at Nixie. More than one blade flashed in the light, and even the whispers reached her ears.

Murderer.

Usurper.

False queen.

Nixie brought her hands in front of her chest and formed a small circle. Inside of it the water swirled, creating a wave not unlike an amplifier the commoners would use. She raised it, and spoke one word, "*Silence!*"

Her voice thundered through the watery cavern, bouncing off walls only to return as a lower but no less savage sound. The raucous crowd quieted. Many of the undines who had been floating above the seats and casting aspersions at Nixie settled back down, instead moving closer to those around them.

Nixie had one chance to get this right, and she knew it. She'd seen leaders speak, she'd seen them lose the faith of an entire people in one wretched moment. The weight of that fact felt like a physical thing pushing down on her shoulders more than the titanic pressure of an entire ocean.

"Many of you are followers of the old traditions. Our last queen was a follower of those traditions. But I think it's important to understand that Lewena is no longer your queen. I harbor no ill will toward any of you who followed her. It shows that you were loyal to the throne, even though the undine who sat upon it was not perfect."

A few murmurs sounded in the stands. A few hooded faces stayed in shadow, revealing nothing about the witches within.

"I only ask you to extend that same opportunity to me. Lewena has fallen, and the world above is changing. I do not know how long you have been here, but if what Pace has told me is true, I know some of you have only recently arrived. And you likely brought news of my ascension to the throne."

"You've come to kill us!" an undine shouted from the back. She stood and pointed toward Nixie, running a hand through her gray-streaked hair. "You murdered our sisters and left them at the bottom of the river. I've seen it. I saw the wreckage you left behind!"

"As is tradition!" Nixie said, biting off each syllable. "You would follow Lewena into oblivion, and yet you deny me my right to defend my allies? My friends?"

"If you're not here to kill us, why are you here? I ask you as Deirdre of the water witches. Faithful to the throne, and the legacy that is rightfully ours."

That was a name Nixie knew. But one she had not heard spoken aloud since the times of Atlantis. She fought off a frown, unwilling to show her surprise in front of the gathered crowd. Deirdre had served the throne long before the fall. She'd been a warrior, an elite guard to the queens, and Nixie was surprised to see her cowering in the ruins of the old city.

"Your reputation is a legend among many of the undines. Why do you hide here?"

"Why do you evade my question?" Deirdre snapped. "I'll grant you the favor of answering yours. I do not hide here, I am here to protect those who have returned. Those who wish to rebuild Atlantis, where it is now, well away from the commoners and the machinations of less savory Fae."

Less savory Fae. Nixie wondered if she meant Nudd, or if perhaps Deirdre was instead referring to her and the other water witches.

Nixie didn't break eye contact with Deirdre, who'd

clearly installed herself as the leader of the deserters. "I've come for the Eye of Atlantis."

Deirdre narrowed her eyes and crossed her arms. "So the blue men did not lie. They've been listening to your conversation with Pace. What ego must you have to return here and simply request one of the most powerful artifacts under undine control."

"It is not ego," Nixie said. "It is necessity, and by right of the crown on my brow."

"What do you need it for?" another undine asked.

"Be silent," Deirdre snapped.

Nixie eyed the two witches for a moment. So they hadn't fully established the leadership among the deserters. That was good. That she could use. She focused on the second witch, a younger witch Nixie doubted was more than half a millennium in age, who squeezed the shoulder of a hooded form beside her.

"I mean to free two of my friends who will die without it. A vampire and a powerful ally—the child who was destined to be the Destroyer, freed from her destiny by the mortal prince of the undines."

A few whispers sounded almost like awe, but Deidre's face twisted in disgust.

"A necromancer has no place in the courts of Faerie, much less among the undines."

"You are wrong," Nixie said. "Perhaps more than

any other, the necromancers understand us. Who else has walked so deeply among the dead? Who else has spoken to the fallen?"

"He stands against the king," Deidre said.

"He stands against the Mad King," Nixie snapped. "Gwynn Ap Nudd seeks to enslave the commoners and bring Faerie to once more rule over their plane."

"Let him do it. What have those fools done for us? Poisoned our waters? Slaughtered the animals who give them sustenance and torn asunder the very flora that gives them breath? They are fools. Let them die."

Nixie offered a small smile. "And how are we so different, sister?"

Deidre flinched as if she'd been slapped, glancing down at the robed witch beside her, face in shadow. "It's not the same."

Nixie frowned. She focused on the hooded forms in the stands. Each silent, each watching, each not wearing traditional dress for the water witches. Or it least it hadn't been since …

"Show me your face," Nixie said, the words not unkind but commanding.

A thick hand reached up to pull their hood back. Deidre grabbed their wrist, stopping the motion. The hooded form shook its head and pushed her away gently. The hood came down, and Nixie gasped.

Beneath waited the sallow cheekbones and long thin beard of a male undine.

"Who … how?" Nixie asked.

The old undine smiled and it lifted the edges of his beard. "My Queen." He inclined his head. "A few of us survived the end of this city. We hid south of here for a time, in ruins far older than Atlantis itself. We only returned five hundred years past."

More hoods fell, revealing at least twelve male undines among the ranks of females.

"You could have been kings," Nixie said, and she didn't hide the confusion in her voice.

"Better to be free than be enslaved to the throne. My name is Shamus."

"You reveal yourself to her?" Deirdre snapped. "She has dishonored that throne. The water witches would surely bow down before a new king before they would ever recognize a betrayer to the throne."

Shamus shook his head slowly. "Deirdre, you are wrong. The queen has ascended to the throne, and she has not broken any laws of our people."

"She is bonded to a mortal. She has made a mortal, a necromancer, a member of the court."

"Only in name," Nixie said. "Damian has no power over our nation. You're well aware of that."

"I am aware of nothing when it comes to you. Other than the fact you betrayed Lewena to her death."

"In that you are wrong. I gifted our allies the fragments of the stone dagger. They had the weapons to strike Lewena down, forged by a fire demon. They saved my life, and that of your mortal prince." She worried she was pushing it too far. But now that she knew they had males among them, who were apparently far slower to rush into a fight, Nixie felt she had more leeway. She hoped she wasn't wrong.

Deirdre didn't respond. She glared at Nixie, even as Shamus reached out and squeezed Deirdre's shoulder.

"Despite the legends around it," Shamus started, "we have no need of the Eye here."

"You're wrong," Deidre said. "The Eye of Atlantis is a symbol of our power. Our legacy. You can't let a traitor to the throne just take it."

"She is no traitor to the throne, Deidre," his voice rising. "She is our queen."

Nixie was surprised when some of the other faces in the audience started nodding along with Shamus. The pieces of what had likely happened here started coming together in Nixie's mind. Shamus was part of the old guard, guardians of kings and queens before the fall. Respected by many, feared by all. But what had softened him over the millennia? For if Nixie hadn't met Damian, or Haka, she might still take nothing but joy in the drowning of the commoners.

"Then you will honor the old ways." Deidre gave one sharp nod as she turned to the other undines in the audience. "Not all here accept her claim. If this so-called queen demands the Eye of Atlantis, she will face me in a battle to the death. The old ceremonies will be observed, and should she be victorious we will acknowledge her as our queen. And should she fail, she will be placed outside the gates to the city as a warning to all."

Nixie grimaced. *Shit.*

CHAPTER SEVEN

S HAMUS LED NIXIE out of the remains of the stadium. Pace followed close behind. They left Deidre in the Coliseum. But it gave Nixie some small hope when she saw some of the water witches left with the blue men, while only a handful stayed with Deidre. But there was no way of knowing how much control Deidre had over them. No way of knowing if they would try to kill her at Deidre's word, or interfere in the coming combat. Nixie remembered coups that struck out at Lewena over the years, and even before that at the kings and queens of old.

"They are young, my Queen. You must forgive them their transgressions."

Nixie assumed Shamus was referring to the handful of youth in the audience. She wondered if he thought Nixie intended to slay them all. As though she were as ruthless as Lewena when she first took the throne, using the deaths of dozens to solidify her rule.

"Deidre doesn't seem very young," Nixie said.

"Yes, yes," Shamus said. "But I think you know it was not Deidre I was referring to. There are water witches here who are not much older than children, by our lifespans."

"I know a wolf who may be even older than you," Nixie said. "A man of peace, an ally whom I would never have believed would one day be an ally."

Shamus looked over at Pace. "I can understand that sentiment."

"Aye," Pace said. "If you'd told me I'd be guarding undines one day, I would've laughed and laughed until I joined my ancestors in oblivion. But here we are. The blue men of the Minch and the undines of old, and we share a fair amount of peace between us."

Shamus inclined his head, and guided them past one of the taller temples that was still intact. It was marble, with highlights of bronze shot through the stone. Nixie couldn't tell who it was meant to worship, but it was an imposing form.

They neared one of the vast stone walls. A large outcropping came close to the edge of the temple they were circling. It wasn't until they reached the wall that Nixie realized a crevasse cut through the stone. This wasn't a neat tunnel like the other they'd walked through. It wasn't like the inverted aqueduct. This was just a shadow in the darkness.

"It's quite stable," Pace said.

"That's not what I was worried about," Nixie said. "Even if these stones collapsed on us, I'd have enough time to escape. But if there were a sword hidden in the dark, I might not."

"You'll find no hidden blades here," Shamus said. "Our confrontations are bald. The time for deception has long passed. I felt no need for it since the city fell, and I believe most of the undines feel the same."

"Lewena poisoned their minds," Nixie said. "She tried to turn a great many of them against us when she wouldn't see reason."

"Reason?" Shamus said with a small laugh. "You yourself would've thought your actions insane a mere millennia ago. Give or take."

There was truth in Shamus's words. And it galled Nixie to remember those times. She still had memories she would consider good of drowning commoners, murdering them. But those memories churned her stomach now, even as she remembered her friends from the past. Times had changed. She repeated the thought out loud. "Times have changed."

"I would not argue that fact, my Queen," Shamus said. "If I could see a way for you to take the Eye without a conflict, I would gladly give it to you. I believe our people have been left too long in the past, in times so poorly remembered they are more legends now than fact."

"There is a great deal of hatred to be overcome," Nixie said. "Even among the Fae, we've grown intolerant."

"That intolerance has lived among the Fae longer than you have been alive. The fact we survive on the same magic, the same blood, matters little to those who see nothing but our differences. And now you wish them to become allies with those who are truly other. Commoners and wolves and vampires. They are not Fae. They are something else."

Nixie blew out a breath. "The Unseelie Fae have made themselves known again. They came hunting an artifact in Kansas City. Attacked the werewolves there, and even engaged the death bats of Camazotz."

Shamus gave a small nod of his head. "If any Fae was to make that kind of shortsighted attack, I would assume it would be the Unseelie."

"Nudd has allied with them," Nixie said.

"That should surprise no one," Shamus said. "If half of what you say about Gwynn Ap Nudd is true, the philosophies of the Mad King are the ideals of the Unseelie Fae."

It made a horrible kind of sense to Nixie. Nudd's words could rally the darkest parts of Faerie. "I've seen the Unseelie cities."

"Then you know how they crush outsiders," Shamus said. "And those they consider outsiders are practically their brothers and sisters. Imagine them unleashed against the commoners."

The crevasse narrowed and they started walking single file, with only a dim golden light to show them the way.

"I think they have an idea." Nixie closed her eyes for a moment and then focused on the light ahead of them. "Nudd stole their most powerful weapons and unleashed the eldritch against the commoners."

"He released eldritch? On the commoners?" Pace asked. "That doesn't seem like a sound strategy."

"They are easily panicked."

"I would not say the loss of one's most powerful weapons is an easy panic," Shamus said. "That would appear to be a logical response to me, if an unwanted one."

"And what would you have them do?" Nixie asked. "You've seen enough of war in your time, I'm sure."

"It is why you find us here," Shamus said. "Hidden away in the ruins of a long forgotten city. I have no need of war. I have no need of killing."

Shamus's words made Nixie wonder if he was already aware of the changes she'd tried to make among the water witches or if it was only a coincidence they shared a view on violence. Tiring of the old ways was certainly not a foregone conclusion. The sheer quantity of Lewena's followers had proven that to Nixie.

"What have you been told about me?" Nixie asked.

"Many things," Shamus said. "And many I hope are true. But surely you must wonder if the very nature of our people *can* change? Our history is not a peaceful one, my Queen. Regardless of what either of us may feel, I'm afraid you cannot escape this challenge. Powerful you may be, the undines here know the old city better than you. To forgo the old ways would be a poor choice. You will not escape Atlantis without a battle."

Nixie smiled in the shadows where no one else could see her. "You need not mistake my intentions. This isn't a confrontation I'd walk away from. And should I lose, give my crown to the victor so they can take their rightful place as the ruler of our people."

"Have you both lost your minds?" Pace asked. "You've either gone as mad as the king, or the witches have truly left the worst of them behind."

"Strange times," Nixie said.

Shamus nodded. "Strange times indeed." They walked in silence for a few minutes, boots occasionally dragging through the silt of the ocean floor and other times floating above it. A brighter light shone at the end of the tunnel before Shamus continued.

"You won't be able to steal the Eye," he said.

"I have no intention of stealing it," Nixie said. "As I already said."

"Of course. But even if you did, it would be impossible to find."

"You don't know where it is," Nixie said. She wondered if perhaps Shamus or even Pace had come to Atlantis looking for the Eye. Or if their motives were as benign as they made it sound. Either way she wasn't getting out of the city without a fight. Perhaps it was time for them to understand just how much she knew.

"The Eye of Atlantis lies beneath the roundtable in the Temple of Poseidon." Nixie's smile grew. "Two rulers before Lewena, she hid it there."

Shamus eyed her. "Perhaps you're the queen after all."

"I don't need your approval."

Shamus turned to face her.

Nixie didn't let him interrupt. "And I don't need your permission. You may be an elder, you could even be from the line of kings thought lost thousands of years ago. But whatever that truth is, you gave up your right to rule. You left your people, left us divided to suffer and find our own way. And here, in the end, we're better for it."

"A queen indeed," Shamus said, his shoulders relaxing. "May your duel end favorably. And now," he said as he stepped aside, "look upon the city that should be yours once more."

Nixie was ready for a sharp reply, but as she stepped out of the tunnel and into a massive section of what once was the center island of Atlantis, she fell into a dead silence. Nixie stared out past the floating lanterns and the warm golden glow they cast onto a city that had been reborn. The walls of the entire cavern from the floor to thirty feet up had been coated in the brilliant golden sheen of orihalchum. She'd seen the commoners use it to strike coins for trade before, but quantities like this were only found in Atlantis.

Every pillar, every doorway, had been polished until it glowed. The Fae lights reflected off of them like a distant firework, and Nixie felt like she was once more stepping into her home. It was something she'd rarely felt since the city fell. And certainly not a feeling she'd had for any mere structure.

"That's impossible," Nixie whispered. "It's like someone just pulled it from the surface and set it here. It's nothing like the ruins we came in through."

"That it is most assuredly not," Shamus said. "If you would've found this place when you visited in the past, it would've looked just as demolished as the outer ruins. We spent a great deal of time cleaning it up."

Nixie shook her head. "This is more than cleaning up. The plating on the stones has been restored. It looks no different than when I lived here. Other than being underwater, of course. What magic did this?"

"Old magic," Shamus said. "Our magic. Though some might say the magic you wish to take away from this place."

Nixie turned to Shamus and frowned. "You're telling me you did this with the Eye of Atlantis? When you don't even know where it is?"

Shamus shook his head. "No, my Queen. This is the magic the undines believed lost long ago from the line of kings. Think of the power of our healers. It was never the kings. That magic has always lived inside every undine, ready to be unlocked. But you have to understand, we don't want to rule. If that means we have to stop drowning a few commoners ... most of us will obey. But the others ..." He shook his head. "We can't tell the others who we are. We simply told them that the magic was drawn from the Eye. It seemed a simple enough lie at the time, but now I'm afraid it may have complicated your plans somewhat."

"It wouldn't be a plan if it actually panned out," Nixie muttered.

Shamus grinned. "Of that we can agree."

Nixie turned away from Shamus, to the city reborn. In the distance, almost like a painting beneath the waves, stood a silver citadel. Golden finials rose up and crowned the Temple of Poseidon. They must have dragged the broken finials in from the old ruins where Nixie had seen them so long ago.

"The arena for duels is not far from the temple, if you would like to take a closer look," Shamus said.

Nixie nodded.

In silence, they started down the central path that led to the temple, each step crossing over tiny stones that formed the countless mosaics telling a history most of the world had forgotten.

CHAPTER EIGHT

N IXIE STOOD IN the entryway to Poseidon's Temple. If she'd had no memory of the last thousand years, she could have believed she was standing inside an undamaged Atlantis. Everything was as it always had been. Other than the occasional fish swimming by.

Her eyes traced the pillars and supports up to the ceiling, shot through with gold, silver, and orichalcum. The roof of the temple had been carved from ivory, long before the commoners had slaughtered enough animals to endanger almost every one that could be harvested for ivory.

Spread out before them, swimming in gold, were hundreds of water witches. They rode upon dolphins as if they were innocent children and not the war dogs of Poseidon. And speaking of the god of the sea himself, he rode upon a golden chariot, looming above his water witches, his nereids.

But that was a sight from time immemorial, a legend passed down from generation to generation until it found its way into the commoners' own lore. If Poseidon had been a true king, he died and faded away, or abandoned his people. In either case, his story lived on, both in the traditions of the water witches and the myths of the commoners.

But there was more to the Temple of Poseidon than even many of the water witches themselves knew. Nixie walked past the opulent dolphins and the glorious witches that rode upon them. Each was carved with detail so intricate one might mistake them for a living being, other than the fact they were solid gold.

Nixie passed beneath the shadow of Poseidon's chariot until she reached the rear wall of the temple. She glanced back at Shamus, who offered no expression. But Pace looked confused. It told Nixie much about the dynamic between the two. Shamus knew exactly what she was doing, but Pace had no idea of the chamber that was hidden beyond.

Nixie's right hand grew translucent and slipped into the crack in the great mosaic of Atlantis. She found the mechanism easily enough, twisted her hand until the handle shifted, and the intricate gearing in the wall clicked into motion. There was a brief rumble, and a small section of the mosaic, barely large enough for a commoner to walk through, sank into the ground.

"What the hell is that?" Pace asked.

Nixie turned back to the passage. "This is where the old kings and queens ruled from and met with their lords and ladies. A safe place, away from prying eyes." She floated forward, letting her hand return to a solid pale flesh color. Dim shadows obscured the room until she crossed the threshold.

Fairy lights burst into golden life. The room was plain, almost unfinished compared to the rest of the temple. But this had never been a place to inspire awe, this was a place where work was done. The massive stone table sat in the center of the room, a simple circle with a complicated rune etched into the surface.

But something was new, and Nixie froze when she saw the stone shelves overflowing with books thought long destroyed.

"From the library?" she asked, eyes widening as she turned back to the tunnel.

Shamus entered the room behind her, followed by Pace.

"They are," Shamus said. "Many books at the old library were warded against damage. Even now, under the sea for over a millennium, they survive."

Nixie ran her finger down one of the spines as she read the title aloud. "Leviticus Aureus and the Fall of Atlantis." She gave a humorless laugh. "I suppose it's only right to have brought one of those here."

"It's one of the few true tellings about what happened," Shamus said. "I thought it should be preserved."

Some of the volumes were written entirely in runes and languages Nixie wasn't familiar with. Damian would have loved to see these. Nixie's hand curled into a fist.

Damian will *see them.*

Nixie turned away from the books. "Lewena knew the Eye was here, but she didn't know more than that. She was never one to believe in the power of a level field, or apparently in what one could learn from books and maps she inherited as queen. She only came here looking for the Eye. Thought it would help unite the water witches, convince them to leave Faerie, but that was a fool's gambit."

"Some would call uniting the water witches a noble cause," Shamus said.

Nixie traced the ancient knotted rune with her index finger. Each seat around the table had a different meaning, a different station in the society of the undines. Even when they tried to show equality by not having a head of a table, they separated everyone, labeled them.

"You rebuilt this room didn't you?" Nixie asked, looking up to Shamus.

Shamus inclined his head. "And you'll find no Eye here. The table itself was broken in half before we repaired it."

"You misunderstand," Nixie said. "I suspect Lewena did too." But Nixie understood as soon as she saw the rune carved into the table. It looked like something Ward would do, only this was far older than the warded man.

Nixie reached out with the gauntlet on her left hand, hovering over a line of runes that almost looked haphazard, and nothing like the intricate Celtic knot that sat on a gray metal disc at the center of the table. But the runes reacted. A silver glow rose, like tentacles of light brushing the gauntlet.

"It needed a key," Shamus said.

"Of a sort," Nixie said, pulling her hand back. "If I lose this duel, I want you both to promise me something."

"We don't owe you anything," Pace said.

Nixie smiled. "Then do not do it for me. Do it because you wish to live here in peace. Do it because you want Faerie to survive the coming war."

"My Queen," Shamus said. "What would you have us do?"

"This gauntlet is the key. The Eye does not rest here. It is in another world, another plane of existence, that you can only reach with this gauntlet. It's what the symbols on the table mean. I never would have understood that until I met a man some time ago."

Shamus backed away a step. "The gauntlet only works if you wear the crown."

Nixie nodded.

"You're asking us to wear the crown?" Pace asked.

"The things you've said, I believe you were both men of peace. Ready for a change among our people. So yes. Should I die, I would like one of you to take the crown. Crush the spirit from the remnants of Lewena's people if you must. But if we do not find peace with the commoners, and the rest of Faerie, I fear not many would survive the coming storm."

Shamus made a disgusted noise. "Then you best not die, Queen. I rid my family of that cursed crown long ago. And I have no intention of taking it back."

Nixie offered the old undine a smile. "We all change, Shamus. All of us."

"We need to get to the arena," Pace said. "Your duel starts soon."

"How do you tell time here?" Nixie asked. "I have no sun to go by, and no mortal watch would survive these depths."

Pace shrugged. "The lights change."

Nixie frowned and looked at the fairy lights around

the room. They'd grown more yellow since they'd entered. Perhaps Nixie had grown too used to the commoners' electricity. She thought they were merely warming up, not marking the passage of time.

"It's not far," Shamus said as he led them out of the hidden room.

Nixie flexed her hands into fists, and the glowing runes faded as she stepped away. She looked once more at the old tomes lining the walls. The other water witches needed to know Atlantis was here. They needed to know they could go home again. But Damian couldn't. Damian was still trapped in the Abyss, and these witches were keeping Nixie from helping him.

A fight was coming. And the rage in Nixie's gut almost sang for it.

CHAPTER NINE

THE ARENA, AS it was called, was small by the standard of most arenas Nixie had seen in her life. It wasn't a full half circle, and there were only about twelve rows of stone seats leading to the top. Each row was carved from a curved section of marble and evenly spaced between one of three sets of stairs.

But the fact the arena wasn't large didn't mean it wasn't full. Water witches and blue men shared the stands, intermingled with no obvious division between who was there to support Nixie, and who rooted for Deirdre.

Nixie's opponent stood at the base of the arena called the orchestra. Deidra waited there, a half step below the pulpit that Shamus had led her in on. Nixie's armor might have been better, as it was the armor of the queen of the undines, but Deidra's would do its job.

Intricate battle scenes and one of the small round flags that marked Lewena's followers adorned Deidra's breastplate. The flattened metal gave a sharp line down to her waist where jointed layers of chainmail would protect against almost any strike. But even through that thick armor, Nixie knew a hard enough blow could do its damage. It would just be a matter of catching her when she wasn't translucent and malleable.

"There's still time to stop this," Deidra said. "Give up the crown you don't deserve."

Nixie shook her head. "I step into this arena of my own free will." She looked up to the stands. "No matter the outcome, remember that we can all change. You live in this place in peace. With no need of drowning the commoners, sinking their ships, stealing their children. Remember that. Remember I did not want this fight. You've chosen your champion. She will fall."

Most of the stands remained silent. And that surprised Nixie. She'd witnessed more than one duel in her time. They were usually rife with taunts and insults. She hoped their silence was a good sign, but she had no way of knowing. She wouldn't know until the fight was over, if she was the one still standing.

The moment Nixie's boot hit the stone surface of the arena, Deidra struck.

Nixie heard the shouts from the crowd then. She heard the gasp from Shamus and the curses from Pace. Deidra's assault may have been unsportsmanlike, but

Nixie had expected it. She parried the blow, smoothly drawing one of her daggers as the water witch sailed by, her sword arcing out to strike at Nixie.

The blade in Nixie's hand tested Deirdre's defenses. She poked and swept and lunged to bait the other water witch. Deidra was skilled, easily dodging the blows and scoring a hit against Nixie's wrist. The metal guard sizzled, and Nixie had no doubt that the blades Deirdre wielded were stone swords.

"You want a world overrun by the Unseelie Fae," Nixie said. "You're a fool."

"And so what if it is?" Deirdre snapped. "Better to serve a ruler who knows their place in the world than bow down to the commoners."

The stands erupted in shouts.

Lewena never wanted that!

You're wrong!

Any Unseelie is better than a traitor!

Nixie glanced at Pace and Shamus. A peaceful hideaway … she thought they had a great deal more work to do.

Deidra grew translucent, her motions harder to follow in the waters around them. But Nixie had been in enough battles to understand where to focus. An undine could elongate her limbs, change her form, but she could not change her weapons. The blade may move at a surprising angle, but it was always attached to the witch.

She saw the lunge, moved to the side, and slammed the hilt of her sword down onto Deidra's hilt. The vibration caused Deidra to stumble and Nixie raised her left hand, summoning a pulse of water to push Deirdre's form away. The whirlpool of force turned the water into a shimmering wavy chaos.

"Yield to me," Nixie growled.

"You won't leave here alive!" Deirdre snarled. "When I'm done with you, I'll drown that prince of yours. Alexandra and Euphemia's heads will hang from—"

Nixie cast her dagger up above Deidre's head. The other water witch watched it as Nixie formed the whirlpool around the dagger, ready to launch it into her opponent. But even as Deidra ranted, Nixie slid the other dagger from her boot and hurled it with the force of a titan. Deidra's breastplate crumpled, the blade cutting deep into her chest before erupting out her back. And there, in that place, the silence was deafening.

Deidra didn't have time to scream. The stone daggers of the queen were far too powerful for that. Her body shifted from a semi-translucent state to a cold gray stone in seconds. The damaged breastplate had curled up inside the stone body, and it would be stuck like that until the end of time.

But that would be a waste of metal. Nixie held her hand out, let the waters spin around Deirdre's frozen form before she said, "Mourn not the lost." She snapped her fist closed and the force of the ocean shattered the undine's form to dust.

Nixie turned slowly toward the spectators, leaning toward them. "Do not mistake my desire for peace as weakness. I have a long memory, and have done many things I would prefer to forget. But I also remember the wars, and how they are won. The world is changing around us. If we do not change with it, we will be lost to history, as much as the kings who came before.

"I'm taking the Eye, but there is something you all need to understand. The Eye is not the magic that sustains this place. That is the deep lines, the ley lines at the bottom of the ocean that feed magicks many of us have forgotten, that live inside each of us. Live here in safety, or join the battle against Nudd." Her voice took on a steel edge. "But do not take up arms against my empire. Or you will fall."

Nixie didn't see who started the chant as she turned to leave. It was only one voice at first. "All hail Nixie!" But more voices joined, and while she was sure the fight with Deidra had left a bitter taste in some of their mouths, it was still good to know she had allies here.

Nixie glanced at Pace as she stepped back up onto the pulpit. "Stay with your people. Tell them what is happening on the surface. They need to know so they can make their own choices about what they want to do."

Pace inclined his head. "Of course, my Queen."

Nixie eyed Pace for a moment. The blue men had always been on the edge of the kingdom of Atlantis, never truly ruled by the queens of old, but never at war with them either. The meaning of those words didn't escape Nixie.

She started back to the Temple of Poseidon, well aware of the presence at her side. He followed her in silence, past the smaller temples and dwellings, until they came once more to the Temple of Poseidon. This time, Nixie noticed where one of the stone offering baskets had been broken away. And she wondered if the basket she'd seen in the other circle of the ruins was the one that belonged to this temple.

Nixie let the thought linger and made her way back into the halls of the temple.

"Well done, my Queen," Shamus said when they crossed the threshold. "I appreciate you not telling them about me. I want no part of that."

"You'll always have a part of that," Nixie said,

clasping his forearm. "Just try to keep them safe. If some of them want to join the battle against Nudd, you can send them back to Giant's Causeway. I have witches there I trust."

"And why is it you trust me?" Shamus asked.

Nixie offered him a small smile as they passed the statues and the golden chariot of Poseidon. "I see much of myself in you. It's a thin line between fighting to change the way our people live, and running away to do the same. You've protected friends and family here, and I suspect you would have done much the same on the surface."

"You can't know that."

"No one really knows ..." Nixie trailed off as she opened the door to the inner sanctum. "No one really knows until they're faced with the choice."

Nixie remembered the shoe that bobbed and sank in the river. She remembered the cries of the boy. A child who would have drowned. Nixie remembered the claws cutting into her skin as that boy was caught between two forms. She remembered the tears on that wolf's face. And Hugh's tears of joy when she brought Haka back to him.

She could have let Haka die that day. Could have torn the breath from his lungs and folded him into the cold embrace of the deeps. But things changed. People changed. And she'd risk everything to show her people a better path.

Nixie held her hand above the table. The runes responded, and this time she didn't pull away. The gauntlet met the table, and brilliant blue light lanced out, racing across the knots and whorls of the ancient ward. If she was right, she'd have the Eye of Atlantis in moments. If she was wrong ... that would be a story for Shamus to tell the next fool.

"No one knows the incantation," Shamus said. "What can you hope to ..."

Nixie smiled and ran two fingers down the back of the gauntlet. A golden streak joined the rich blue light of the ward, and darkness took her.

CHAPTER TEN

NIXIE'S HEART HAMMERED in her chest. She'd been confident, but confidence didn't always mean survival. A pinprick of golden light grew on the horizon and something like relief washed over her.

She turned, and was met by the vision of a floating jewel, no larger than an eye. More light blossomed around her, and the blackness of the Abyss changed. It took on a deep red color that undulated and shifted against the golden motes.

"Get out!" a voice screamed, shattering the silence and echoing into eternity.

An eye opened beside her, blood red and shot through with darkness. Its twin joined it before she saw the horns below, the distended limbs and a mouth so full of fangs it was a wonder it could even close.

"Fuck!" Nixie shouted, snatching the blue eye out from where it floated amid the wall of awakening fire demons. It was a cold thing that made the void of the Abyss feel warm. But even as the thought crashed through her mind, she realized the heat was coming from above. A torrent of flame, unleashed by the horned head of a titanic demon.

Her hair singed as she dragged two fingers down the back of the gauntlet. The flesh of her right arm blistered as she held it up to shield herself. There was no water here. No power for her to defend herself with. But nothing would stop her so long as she drew breath.

The gauntlet stuttered, and the world roared around her.

Darkness became light, and the waters boiled around her. Nixie's own scream was deafening as sound returned. She clutched the scorched flesh of her right arm and collapsed onto the top of the round table.

✦　✦　✦

"DON'T MOVE," A voice said.

Nixie bristled at the sound, and then winced as her muscles tightened. Was this it? Were they going to strike her down while she was weak?

"I know it may be a bit nasty, but I promise it can heal the worst burn from a fire demon."

Nixie cracked an eye open and found Shamus standing over her, smearing some kind of hideous orange poultice on a kelp bandage before wrapping it around her hand.

"The Eye?" she asked, but her voice was cracked, dried out like a desert plain.

Shamus winced and picked up a foul-smelling jar floating beside him. "Must have inhaled a bit of that fire." He frowned and studied her face. "Well, I have good news, and I have bad news."

Nixie narrowed her eyes.

"Oh, it's not that bad." Shamus spooned a heaping dollop of orange gunk out of the jar in his hand. "Just swish it around a bit and swallow it."

If he'd been trying to kill her, feeding her poison at this point probably wouldn't have been the approach. She opened her mouth wider and almost cried as the flesh split at the corners of her lips. And Mike wondered why undines generally didn't like fire demons.

"What is it the commoners say?" Shamus asked. "Here comes the aeroplane?"

Nixie couldn't stop the pained laugh. Shamus gently scraped the spoon off on her teeth, careful not to touch her split skin. She chewed and swished the viscous stuff and her mouth felt better instantly, until her brain registered the taste.

"By the gods!" she muttered through a grimace. "It's like a rotten lobster left out in the sun for a week."

"Always thought it was more like two weeks,"

Shamus said. "Don't forget to swallow it. Take some water in, too. Let it fill your lungs."

Nixie stopped swishing, closed her eyes against the horrifying lumpy texture, and swallowed. The torn flesh mended in her throat and lungs under the care of the wretched stuff, but she couldn't stop gagging on the rotten fish taste.

Shamus applied another of the bandages on the side of Nixie's face. "You know, my father always wanted me to be an alchemist. That was never my true calling. A healer, now that was something I could be proud of. My mother died in one of the old wars, but I always thought she would have been proud, too."

"I never knew my parents," Nixie said. Her voice was returning, but she still flinched at the awful taste.

"Never?" Shamus asked. "Well, that's rather sad, I must say. But you still had a family, I assume?"

"Euphemia." Nixie offered a weak smile. "She was all the sister I ever needed, and later we met Alexandra."

Shamus nodded and peeled back some of the older bandages. "We all have family, whether we realize it or not. Those who would fight for us, and sometimes those who live for us."

Nixie turned and looked at Shamus, studying the lines of the old undine's face. "Who are you?"

"A humble healer. Now rest. You've had quite a rough day getting the Eye."

Nixie's heart pounded in her chest. "Where is it?"

"Right where you left it." Shamus held up Nixie's gauntlet and unfolded it. Nestled in the center was the brilliant blue orb of the Eye of Atlantis. "You know, you would not have survived the trial without your love for the necromancer."

"What?" Nixie asked, furrowing her brow and wincing as she felt the skin split.

Shamus adjusted the bandage on her head. "Though I'm afraid you still hold a fair amount of hatred in your heart. Hence the burns."

"What trial?"

"Well," Shamus said, "perhaps you were luckier than I imagined. It is not unusual for the Fae to protect sacred artifacts with a trial to test the heart of the one who seeks it."

"I've heard stories, but ... I thought they were only stories."

"Just as Atlantis is only a story to a great many who live upon this world. There is truth in most tales, my Queen. You need only seek it out. Now, the trials of the Fae were rather ingenious, I always thought. To retrieve the Eye of Atlantis, you must hold more love within your heart than hatred. But other trials would test your knowledge, bravery, or trust."

"I know the stories. So no one Fae could wield too much power. A Fae filled with love may still hold fear, so he would never be able to suffer the trials of two."

"Not just stories, though," Shamus said. "It would do my Queen well to remember that."

"It would have done your queen better to warn her," Nixie muttered.

Shamus grinned and removed another bandage. He reached out and gently tilted her head from one side to the other. "Not much else I can do. Our regular healing incantations don't work so well when the damage is caused by a fire demon. And just in case you get any ideas of asking someone to heal you right now, don't."

"I know," Nixie said. "The flames of fire demons leave a mark for a time. If someone tried to heal me more than you already have, the spell would backfire and consume them instead."

"Exactly," Shamus said. "So don't go asking for more help than you already have. You need to wait at least a few hours."

A few hours didn't seem so bad. But they had been in the middle of the battle, a wound like the one she had just suffered could've meant her end, or the end of a well-meaning healer. Fire demons and water witches were incompatible at the most basic levels of existence.

Which made her friendship with Mike the demon all the more strange.

Nixie sat up and swung her legs over the edge of a spongy bed. It probably would have been simple to float, but she'd spent enough time on the surface that sometimes she felt better with stone beneath her boots.

She looked around the small gilded room and realized she was in one of the domiciles nestled inside the Temple of Poseidon. Where the main hall was coated in gold and precious metals, this room was simpler. A small bookcase sat in the corner along with a cage Nixie suspected held live snacks.

"Hungry?" Shamus asked as he followed her gaze.

"I can't fully express to you how *not* hungry I am after eating that … paste."

"Have you ever had fish paste? A strange concoction the commoners came up with. I'm rather fond of it myself." Shamus gave her a broad smile before pulling the last of the bandages away from her face. He frowned and nodded. "Not too bad. Once a healer can get to you, I doubt you'll have so much as a scar leftover. You did well, my Queen."

Nixie ran a hand through her hair, wiping away the last of the salve before she picked up her crown and set it on her brow.

Shamus picked up the armor and greaves from the table beside the bookshelf. "Allow me."

Nixie nodded and waited as Shamus strapped her armor gently onto her healing flesh. The cold metal felt good against the residual burn. He moved to her greaves, and as the last buckle fastened, the armor glowed as it covered the joints in magic.

Shamus took a knee, which made Nixie remarkably uncomfortable in the small room. "My Queen, should you have any need." He held out a tiny disc. It was the smallest Wasser-Münzen she'd ever seen.

"And you. If I can come, I will. And I promise you I'll return here one day. Even if it is only my armor, returned by the Morrigan."

A sad smile crossed Shamus's face. "I hope you can change the world, my Queen. We've been hiding and dying for far too long."

And killing. Nixie thought the words, but she didn't speak them aloud. "As the war rages above, do not be surprised if Nudd sends the eldritch things to attack Atlantis."

"Do not be surprised if there, at the end of times, you find allies at your side you did not expect."

Nixie studied the Eye of Atlantis on her palm before locking it away in a pouch at her side. Shamus held up her sword, which she took and sheathed at her waist.

With that, Nixie left the Temple of Poseidon, swimming once more through the crevasse and ruins, greeting a few curious faces as she left Atlantis behind.

✦   ✦   ✦

THE TRENCH WAS dark once more as Nixie took to the sea and began her ascent. It didn't quite feel real that she'd set foot in Atlantis. That undines were living there, deep beneath the sea. Memories of her time spent in Atlantis above the ocean warred with what she'd seen today.

She drifted silently, until she reached a depth where the anglerfish prowled once more, and the dim lights of their lures brightened like the stars of the Abyss. Their jagged teeth reminded her of the fire demon she'd seen. It was unlike any she'd encountered in their wars. The basic shape was somewhat reminiscent of Mike's true face, but it was so different, so much … darker.

Nixie shivered as something brushed by her. Her armor brightened with a tiny effort of will, bringing to life a small light incantation to see where she was going. The wall of the trench surprised her with its proximity, but then it moved.

The massive form swiped its tail and bumped her again before she saw the eye.

"Guardian," Nixie said with a small smile, reaching out to pat the enormous snout of the Mosasaurus.

ERIC R. ASHER

Gradually the dark of the ocean gave way to the dim light of the sun overhead, and that dimness gave way to the blue of the seas, and a brilliant warmth. She broke the surface a long way from the forts on the northern shore of Puerto Rico.

Nixie could have used the gauntlet then and there without issue, but she remembered the fire demons in the darkness, and she wanted to be far away from the place that had taken her to them. She shivered and glided over to the Mosasaurus, ready to hitch a ride back to the shallows. Besides, he'd be handy to have around if they encountered any more leviathans.

She rode on the back of the guardian, nestled between the base of his skull and the smooth scales that made excellent footholds. It wasn't long before the sun started to drift farther toward the horizon, and the shadow of San Morro grew larger.

But Nixie and the guardian weren't alone in the waters below the fort. Shattered hulls and the wreckage of a fishing boat floated by. At first she thought it was leftover debris from their earlier battle, but there was too much. They were just close enough to the shore to see the figures standing on the shoals when she heard the voice, and her grip tightened on the guardian.

"Hand over the Eye of Atlantis or we'll bury the rest of the commoners in the bay."

CHAPTER ELEVEN

THE GRAY FLESH of the Fae standing on the shoals caught Nixie off guard. She knew the Unseelie Fae had returned. She'd been warned. Her allies had faced them in the ruins of Quindaro. But to see them in the flesh after they'd spent so much time in the shadows …

As if on cue, screams went up from the channel. Nixie snapped her gaze to another fishing boat as the mast crumbled and the hull shattered. But it didn't stop there. The ship exploded, splinters erupting into the air on a geyser. If any commoner had been on that boat, they were dead.

The Unseelie Fae raised his hand to the heavens and another fairy appeared above him, standing at the edge of the fort. From the watchtower, he extended his arm and a young boy screamed as he first tried to pull away from the Fae, before he realized he was dangling dozens of feet above the rocks below.

"The choice is yours," the Unseelie Fae said.

Nixie assessed the Fae, and the likelihood of saving

the child. The Unseelie were known for their ruthlessness. And that was something of note among the Fae.

"The Eye of Atlantis is yours." The rage Nixie was trying to keep hidden was betrayed by her armor. Bright red bolts of power lanced down her arm as she reached into the pouch at her side and raised the Eye for them to see.

She stepped off the Mosasaurus's back and let the water carry her toward the shore. The guardian growled behind her, the violent promise in that sound sending a chill down Nixie's back.

"And they call you a queen," the Unseelie Fae said. "Why they ever feared a water witch is beyond me. Docile creatures, aren't you? Servants who know your place?"

Nixie smiled at the Fae. Ten feet from the shoals was close enough. She slid the Eye back into the pouch at her side as the next wave crashed against the shoals. A stream of water continued up the side of the fort, slithering through the cracks and crevices until it reached the fairy dangling the child, promising his death.

The water lashed out, mortar exploding from the old fort. Stone that had not seen the light of day in centuries shot skyward, cutting through the fairy's groin, arms, and face. The child screamed as the ruined flesh collapsed in front of him. But that deadly water changed, extended, and caught the boy, pulling him back into the watchtower.

Nixie sent her voice through that water to scream a warning to everyone standing upon the fort. "Run!"

The Unseelie Fae crashed onto the walking path below, a crumbled, bloody heap as his body collapsed in on itself and a terrifying tortured scream rose out the ruined armor.

"General?" one of the other Fae asked.

The speaker who had threatened Nixie responded. "Unleash the leviathans! Soak the commoners in the blood of her ignorance."

The water of the bay churned and boiled. Tentacles as thick as trees rose and chased more of the fishing vessels. Even those who had retreated far into the bay weren't safe.

Water cascaded down the backs of leviathans as tentacles shot out to the shore and found purchase to drag themselves close to the docks.

"Go!" Nixie shouted to the Mosasaurus. "Protect the commoners as if they were your wards!"

"The great guardian of Atlantis," the general said with a hollow laugh. "You're outmatched, queen. You could have worked with us, embraced your true self, helped us drown these commoners in an orgy of your power."

Every word sent a frisson of rage through Nixie's body, and the Eye pulsed in her pocket. She swept her arms up to the side, and the ocean responded like it was the wings of a goddess, carrying her skyward.

Nixie unsheathed the sword at her waist and leveled it at the general. "You'll die last." She shifted the blade to the Fae standing beside him, and the ocean moved. Red lightning crackled from her armor, lancing out through the water and bathing the entire scene in an eerie red glow. She surged forward.

The soldier raised his sword to block Nixie's incoming strike, but it shattered when her stone sword swept through it and relieved him of his head. Her foot caught the edge of a shoal, twisted, and she lunged for the next. She impaled two of the fairies on her blade and used the ocean water to pull them down as their screams began.

Shouts drew Nixie's attention back to the fort. She let the ocean carry her to the wall, leaving the general to scramble away from a tower of water crashing onto the shore. A smooth arc carried her to the top of the battlements where the Unseelie Fae had dangled the child.

In the distance, the world shook as the guardian unhinged his jaws and roared. Teeth locked into a leviathan that had reached one of the cruise ships. Nixie could hear the rubbery snap of flesh from the top of the fort before the Mosasaurus spun violently and tore the leviathan away.

The tentacles reached for the guardian, but another chomp of its mighty teeth stilled the leviathan. As soon as the creature lay motionless, the Mosasaurus sped off through the water, seeking its next victim. It created a huge wake as it went, threatening to capsize the smaller boats, but Nixie had other things to worry about at the moment.

At the top of the fort waited a small squadron of Unseelie Fae. These weren't like the soldiers the general had stood with on the shoals below. At least two of them were knights, their powers given away by the frost running along their gauntlets.

To slay a knight would be to make an enemy of that knight's court for eternity. Nixie remembered the warnings and stories in the books from Atlantis. And then she remembered the atrocities the Unseelie Fae had committed, and would commit again.

Her eyes widened as the power coursed through her armor, sending her hair into a wild halo behind her. The choice was made. They would all die here.

Every.

Her sword reached the first impossibly fast.

Last.

The knight's confused look didn't change as his severed head hit the ground.

One.

The jet of ocean water hit the third hard enough to pulp her gray flesh, sending a ruin of gore to splash down beside the clattering armor of her allies.

Nixie ground her teeth together as more screams sounded from the floor above her. The last knight was not so easy a target. By the time Nixie reached him, he already had an icy shield prepared to parry her blow.

Even as she rebounded off the knight's defenses, the knight attacked. A foot-long spike of frozen water crashed into a weak spot on Nixie's armor. The magic flexed and bent but it did not break. But she hadn't been expecting it. Her arm had still been solid inside the armor, and she could feel the wound.

The knight struck again, and Nixie deflected the worst of the blow, but an icy blade still cut into her cheek. It felt as if the blade was going to suck the life from her very body just from that tiny wound. A horrid chill coursed through her, so much so she almost wished she could be in the presence of the heat of the fire demons once more.

Screams sounded again. Nixie cursed, focused her will, and a cannon shot of water pushed the knight off the side of the fort. Nixie doubted very much it would be enough to kill him, but would give her enough time to get up the stone ramp, through the tunnel, and see what the hell was happening.

She sprinted through the darkness and broke into the early evening sun. It looked like it was only commoners huddled there.

"What's wrong? What's happened?"

"There's a thing …" an older man started, his voice shaking. "A thing on the grounds outside the fort, killing people, Miss. It's not safe."

"Where they fly kites?"

The man nodded.

Nixie cursed and sprinted past a family holding their child. "You all need to get out of here. It's not safe. Get back to the city! I'll make you a path!"

None of them moved as Nixie reached the far archway, but the Mosasaurus bellowed in the distance, and the earth-shaking sound was enough to startle them into motion.

Nixie hurdled the outer edge of the fort, crashing down onto a narrow wall before she saw it.

"Fuck me, what the hell is that?"

A blob, for that was the only name she could give it, a mass of teeth and arms and legs that surged and compressed as it undulated across the grounds. It had no logical form. A hundred mouths gnashed their all too human-like teeth as broken and maimed limbs scratched at the ground, dragging it forward.

Nixie almost vomited when she saw it catch a commoner. The man's body just ... came apart, absorbed into the eldritch thing in an instant. Another mouth, another pair of legs, and a streak of blood appeared, flowing through a new tangled mass of vessels.

A third leviathan appeared offshore to the north, and despair knifed its way into Nixie's heart. This couldn't be stopped. There were too many. It was too much.

She could go, get the Eye to Zola. Maybe they could save Damian. But could she live knowing she abandoned all these people? These commoners lived on the edges of Atlantis, they were *her* people, even if they didn't know it.

And before she was sure of what she was doing, her legs carried her in a mad rush toward the vile creature leaving death and ruin in its wake. Long enough they'd been hidden in the shadows.

The Eye pulsed in her satchel.

Long enough she'd stood by and tried to speak sense into her enemies.

Her hand slid into the pocket without knowing

why.

Long enough they'd been subjected to cruelty at the hands of a mad ruler.

Warmth flowed into the chilled wounds the knight had inflicted.

Long enough they'd stood by as the world devoured itself.

The scream that rose from Nixie's throat wasn't hers. The magnificent arches of water that erupted from either side of the fort weren't her own. This was an old power, an ancient thing meant to test the heart of a ruler.

Two hundred eyes swiveled toward her as the translucent mass lost its focus on devouring commoners. Nixie's cry fractured into the thundering scream of a goddess, and searing red lightning leapt from her blazing armor, lighting the incoming water with the rage of an entire people.

The ocean crashed down around her, and the eldritch being screamed from a thousand mouths that weren't its own. Lightning pummeled the beast and water crushed it into the surface of the grass.

She heard the cries behind her, her body turning slowly to see the cowering people behind her.

"Run!" she said, but her voice sounded wrong, too loud, too confident. "I'll hold it back, but you have to *run!*"

A young girl went first, the determination on her tan face an unspoken promise to the baby bundled in her arms.

The creature tried to move, but Nixie closed her hands into fist, sending a shower of blood red lightning into the thing's body.

More commoners ran. People she would have dragged to the bottom of the sea not a century ago, and that guilt awoke a rage inside her she could not contain.

Nixie's scream was joined by more voices, and she stared in awe as figures sprang from those waters. Undines crashed to the earth around the fleeing commoners, running beside them, slaughtering any Unseelie Fae foolish enough to stand in their way.

The seas shook, and the silvery flashes of the tails of the blue men of the Minsch flickered through the waters, scooping up commoners and delivering them to the shores.

Nixie raised her voice to the sky, her head shaking as she came to understand the power of the Eye. It would have burned her to ash if she'd been unworthy. It's why the Eye was never wielded as a weapon. No witch had ever been prepared to take the risk. Never prepared to change their nature.

The last of the commoners ran to the relative safety of Old San Juan.

"You can't kill it," the general said from behind her.

Nixie closed her eyes, and the towering arches of water shifted, erupting beneath the eldritch thing and tossing it into the ocean like it weighed nothing.

The Mosasaurus surged to the surface, distracted from its prey as though it had heard Nixie's signal. The horrible blob vanished into the guardian's jaws. A long time ago, in ages forgotten, it was a great honor to be sacrificed to the guardian. Nixie hoped those people might find some peace in that, however small.

"What are you?" the general asked, backpedaling as Nixie turned toward him, red lightning sparking across her gauntlets.

The winds shifted, the ocean having upset the air so badly a tropical storm was forming above them. Nixie looked out at the bay. Pace dragged a life raft to shore in the distance, avoiding the dismembered tentacles floating on the water.

"I am Nixie of Atlantis, Queen of the Undines. Should you set foot upon these lands or waters again, you will meet a most unfortunate end."

The knight struck from Nixie's blind spot. She felt the chill as the icy dagger cut into her hand, one of the only unarmored spots on her body. He tried to follow it up with an incantation, but the ice met a wall of boiling water.

"An unfortunate end," she repeated, and that wall of boiling water snapped closed around the knight, cutting him off from the ley lines, preventing him from escaping. Nixie raised her head slightly and stared at the knight.

He screamed, and as he screamed, she forced the boiling tower down into his lungs until they could hold no more. Organs ruptured, eyes collapsed, and his body expanded until it burst.

"It will be worse for you," Nixie said, turning to the general as she let the knight's screaming armor collapse to the earth in a pool of gore before it returned to the lines.

The general didn't speak. He slashed at the air and vanished into the Warded Ways.

CHAPTER TWELVE

"**W**ELL, THAT'S DISGUSTING."
Nixie turned to find Shamus studying the empty armor of the knight. Something huge and wet crashed together and Nixie caught a glimpse of the Mosasaurus snuffling through the ruin of a leviathan.

She looked down at the Eye of Atlantis in her hand. "Was that all the Eye?" Water ran off the grasslands, dripping onto the walking paths before it trailed back into the sea.

"Not entirely," Shamus said. "That was the armor and crown of the queen who has accepted her station. I have not seen such a display in a very long time."

Nixie turned back to the bay. "Is he just going to eat all of the leviathans?"

Shamus laughed. "I imagine he's rather hungry after hibernating for a millennium. I doubt he'll eat all of those creatures. Some will settle to the bottom of the ocean and feed the wildlife there. It is a cycle that will continue until the end of this world."

Nixie rolled the Eye of Atlantis between her fingers and thumb. "How did you know I needed help?"

"The Eye of Atlantis bound you to the city."

"What?" Nixie asked.

The old man grinned. "We knew the island was in danger because of the Wasser-Münzen you carry. You drew on the ley lines through it, hard enough to move the earth. The mountain did not break away, the land did not shift and destroy the homes of the commoners as it could have. But it did reveal parts of Atlantis that had been lost. There is more now to see in the outer ring. More for us to rebuild. Perhaps, when this conflict is done, you may return?"

"I'd like that," Nixie said as she slid the Eye of Atlantis back into the pouch at her side. It clicked against the coin there. "I'd like to see what else you saved in that bookshelf."

"Then I will be sure to keep it safe for you."

The guardian clamped down on one of the last large chunks of the leviathan and dragged it beneath the surface. The wake of the Mosasaurus sent small waves rushing toward the shore, and made the blue men bob among the rocks. Pace was there.

Nixie exchanged a nod with Shamus and then started down toward the shore.

"We'll meet again, my Queen. And may it be a time

of peace."

"Just don't drown anyone in the meantime," Nixie shouted back. "Unless they really deserve it."

Shamus's laugh followed Nixie as her boots cracked onto the walking path and then gave way to the silt of the shore.

A commoner stood on the shore, not far from Pace on the other side of the shoals. She didn't look panicked or shocked by the presence of the blue man, which likely meant she wasn't what she seemed, or that Pace had saved her.

"That's her," Pace said to a soaking wet bundle in his arms. He pulled down the edge of a blue hoodie, revealing the face of a girl who couldn't have been more than seven.

"She was injured when two of the ships collided," Pace said, turning the child toward Nixie. "I did what I could, but the incantation had ... side effects."

The girl pulled her hoodie down again for a minute, took a deep breath, and then unzipped it to show Nixie her neck. A brilliant blue streak glowed in the girl's flesh, translucent enough she could see the blood pumping through her veins.

Nixie pursed her lips. "That's different."

"I've never tried to heal a human before. Did I do it wrong?"

"She's alive," the woman beside them said. "I don't care what you did wrong. You did that right."

"You're like a princess," the girl said. "That's what Base said."

"Not ... exactly." But Nixie couldn't stop the smile that slid across her face. "Base?"

"She has trouble with her Ps," the woman said.

"May I try something? A healing ... technique?" Nixie waited for the woman's response.

"Come on, Mom," the girl said.

"Sure, of course. You people ..." her eyes trailed down to Pace's fins, gracefully twitching in the waves. "You saved us already. I trust you."

"You shouldn't always trust the Fae," Nixie said. "Some of them have ill intentions."

"Like your king?" the mom asked. "He rubs me the wrong way. People shouldn't be killing each other, but stealing those weapons was no way to make peace."

"He's not my king," Nixie said, reaching out to the girl.

"Is it going to hurt?" she asked, leaning back against Pace.

"No more than it already hurts," Nixie said. "You might be tired, though. That's normal. Are you ready?"

She nodded, but Nixie could see the tears in the corners of the girl's eyes.

"*Socius Sanation.*" The incantation wasn't much

above a whisper, but the child's gasp was like thunder. White light that gave off no illumination glowed all around them, casting Nixie's fingers and the blue flesh into a dim gray.

And then it was over. A hint of blue remained on the girl's throat, but Nixie couldn't see the veins and lifeblood pulsing beneath her skin. She took a deep breath and nodded to the girl.

"All done."

"Done?" she asked, cracking open one eye.

"Yes, now let's get you back to your mom."

Pace gently raised her to Nixie when the flash burst around them. And then another as Nixie set the girl down just on the edge of the shore by her mother, but she wouldn't let go of Nixie's hand.

She turned back and said, "Thank you, Base."

The blue man of the Minch nodded to her. "Of course, princess."

The girl grinned, squeezed Nixie's hand, and reached out to her mother. Another flash of light and Nixie squinted at the commoner some twenty feet away. A brilliant flash from the man's camera threatened to blind her.

"Reporters," Nixie groaned.

"Are you really a queen?" the girl asked, looking up at Nixie from her place beside her mom.

"I am, child."

"I'm a princess."

Her mom squeezed her child's shoulders. "Thank you. Get out of here. I'll talk to the reporter."

"You don't have to do that," Nixie said.

"And your people didn't have to save us," she said. "You didn't have to save my princess. Now go."

With that, the mom and her child walked toward the reporter.

The Mosasaurus roared in the distance.

"Rest well, guardian," Nixie said as the earth vibrated beneath her feet.

"Until we meet again," Pace said with an awkward salute off his eyebrow.

"Thank you, friend. Until then."

The blue man vanished into the waters.

"Would you *please* let me by?" a raised voice shouted.

Nixie saw the reporter, blocked in by the dancing child and her admirably stubborn mother. Nudd and the Unseelie Fae had dared to attack commoners on the ancient shores of Atlantis. That would not stand.

She took a deep breath as exhaustion settled in. Two fingers ran down the back of the gauntlet on Nixie's left hand. For a moment she feared what might be waiting for her in the shadows, but whatever it was, she'd be ready.

The Abyss opened its arms once more.

CHAPTER THIRTEEN

THE GOLDEN PATH materialized between one step and the next. No cage appeared. No long savage teeth of the fire demon's face. Instead, it was just the darkness of the Abyss, and the dim lights in the distance.

Nixie felt the tug, but the path before her did not change. Instead, a small shower of golden lights drifted down beside her until footsteps echoed hers, and the glowing form of Gaia took shape.

"Is Damian okay?" Nixie asked. "Did something happen?"

"He is as well as he can be," Gaia said. "You need not worry yourself more."

That was good to hear, but even if he was as well off as he had been before, that wasn't exactly a good thing. He was still trapped in the Abyss, still trapped in the corrupted mantle of Anubis. And he would be until they could transfer Gaia's powers, but even that had no guarantees.

"Your journey was a success?" Gaia asked.

Nixie felt it had been more of a statement than a question, but she answered regardless. "I got the Eye. I'm taking it to Zola now. Hopefully she's still at Coldwater."

"Her journey will perhaps be the hardest of them all."

"Why?" Nixie asked. "Why is Zola burdened with anything more than the rest of us?"

"Because she takes the guilt for all that has happened onto herself," Gaia said. "But these things are not her fault. Perhaps one day she will be able to understand that. But for now, that guilt fuels her, drives her to the end of her path."

"What else do we need to save Damian?" Nixie asked.

"The items you have gathered thus far will assist in saving Vicky, and Damian's sister, Samantha. Once Zola acquires the third piece, the cores of the blood knot can be transferred. Should she fail, then the gift of my powers to Damian will kill both of them."

Nixie cursed under her breath. "It would be great if for one damn time the consequences weren't life and death."

Gaia offered her a warm smile. "That is all the world is."

Nixie sighed. "I suppose it is."

"But I have not visited you merely to discuss philosophies. I am afraid Damian's time is limited."

"What do you mean?" Nixie looked up at the goddess when she didn't answer.

"His consciousness is fading," Gaia said. "I cannot feel much of who he is anymore. I believe the Abyss has slowed the effect, but you do not have long."

"How long?" Nixie asked.

"It is impossible to say exactly," Gaia said. "But it would seem the magic of the Mad King has damaged the mantle more than we realized." Gaia closed her eyes and turned her head skyward for a moment. "There are still many souls trapped within him, many voices, and I think they have given him some anchor. But they are being pulled away, and I do not think he has more than a few days."

Nixie cursed. "We need the last core."

"Yes," Gaia said, "but that is not all we will need to transfer my powers to Damian. That is what you need to spare the life of Samantha and Vicky. The cores and an anchor to bind the three."

"That has to be our priority," Nixie said. "Damian wouldn't be able to live with himself if those two died." Her own words cut deep into her heart. But she knew it was true. That wasn't the kind of thing he'd come back from. That would bury him in agony until the end of his days.

"Be quick, my Queen, for time has grown short. Find a worthy anchor for their life-force."

Nixie blinked at Gaia's use of her title. "Do what you can to keep him here. Keep him safe."

"Be wary," Gaia said. "Gwynn Ap Nudd has escalated the forces he's sending against you. The chaos you fought outside the fort was a mere reflection of what that monster can be. Be wary."

Nixie felt the tug on her being from the gauntlet, telling her she was at her destination. She slowed to a stop and Gaia hovered beside her, the golden motes of her eyes studying Nixie for a time.

"I've seen much change in the world and the time I have lived. But perhaps the change in you, and your people, has surprised me more than any. I wish you well on your journey, my Queen. Protect your people and do not forget you have many allies."

"Thank you." She inclined her head and swiped her fingers across the back of the gauntlet. The Abyss shimmered, and Nixie fell.

CHAPTER FOURTEEN

I T WASN'T A smooth exit from the Abyss. Nixie frowned at the sudden feeling of weightlessness until her vision returned and she saw the water rushing up to greet her. A muffled curse escaped her lips as she splashed down into a pond filled with some very surprised looking frogs.

Nixie glided to the edge of the water and climbed out of the blue pool. A small patch of algae stuck to her shoulder and she peeled it off with some irritation. Something wiggled near her waist and she looked down to find a bulky frog nestled between her satchel and her armor.

She held her hand out and scooped up the little amphibian. It was then that she remembered the pond, remembered talking to Damian as he stood on the shore not far from where she was. She'd done a water sending, and one of those little frogs had gotten sucked up into it. Nixie smiled at the memory and set the squishy green lump back into the pond.

Coldwater was a strange place. On the surface it was peaceful, tranquil even. But something was unsettling about the old fields. Demons had been slain here. Necromancers, commoners, and the ghosts of all of them prowled the shadows.

Nixie stepped through the tall weeds at the pond's edge and started toward the cabin that sat on a short hill in the distance. She frowned at the sun, higher in the sky than it had been in the Caribbean. Traveling great distances was far more jarring near sunrise and sunset.

The green tin roof caught the light and the old oak in the front yard looked like an inferno in the reflection. A copperhead snake raised a curious head above the grass before vanishing once more into the undergrowth. They were venomous serpents to commoners, but harmless to the undines.

Nixie ran her hand along the tips of some tall purple flowers, an unnatural color to see in this part of the state, but she knew what lay buried beneath her feet. The remains of a demon, the one known as Azzazoth. It was a story Damian liked to tell, and one Nixie had heard far too many times. She only hoped she'd get to hear it again.

Startling Zola Adanaya was to invite a terrible death. Nixie let her boots thump hard on the wooden steps leading up to the screen door. Gray shingles hung across the wall and a mangled rusty chair sat in the corner.

Nixie pulled the screen door open, and it squealed like a piglet. She pushed through the door behind it and stepped into the cabin. The conversation in the front room died.

"Girl," Zola said, tapping her knobby old cane on the hardwood floor, "I've seen three-days dead raccoons that looked better than you."

Nixie gave a weak smile. "It's been a rough day."

Motion on the coffee table drew her attention. Aideen was there, camped out on a miniature bench next to Zola's coffee mug.

"Did Mike do that?" Aideen asked.

"What? No! Mike would never do this." Nixie traced the lines of rough flesh along her right cheek. "It was another fire demon. Several of them, actually. A trial guarding the Eye of Atlantis." She prodded at her other cheek, but the wound from the Unseelie knight had already healed.

An old black and white television sputtered in the corner opposite a wood stove. The words from the reporter drew Nixie's attention and she blinked at the image.

"Once again, we haven't confirmed this is the wife

of infamous necromancer Damian Vesik, but that is the current belief."

Nixie frowned at the television. "Excuse me? I have a *name*."

"Not to mention a title," Aideen muttered.

"This photo shows the mother and daughter rescued outside the fort called Del Morro in Puerto Rico. When asked for comment, the mother tripped our local reporter. Sadly, the queen vanished. But this shows you what we've been saying for weeks now at Channel 15 News: the Fae are as multifaceted as we are. They aren't all your enemies. And if you slip back into a hatred of all Fae, remember this photo." He pointed to the small rectangle floating above his shoulder. "Remember that she killed those monsters and saved that family. Never forget it."

The photo took up the whole screen now, showing Nixie hand in hand with that mother and daughter, Pace just a blur in the background. But the gratitude on the woman's face was plain to see, and the admiration caught in the little girl's smile cut Nixie to the bone.

Her façade fractured and she covered her face with her right hand. Tears fought their way free no matter how hard she resisted them. Nixie bit the inside of her mouth, dug her nails into her palm, but nothing could stem the tide.

Something slammed into her as she stood on the orange area rug and wept. Nixie opened her eyes and found a teenager with hair like an inferno wrapped around her waist.

"I'm glad you're here," Vicky said. "It's kind of like Damian's here, too."

Nixie tried to speak, but only a sob came out. She crushed Vicky in a hug. A firm hand squeezed her shoulder and she didn't need to see the old necromancer to know it was Zola.

"Oh god, my feels," another voice said from the kitchen.

Nixie looked past the little bar and gave a shaky laugh when she saw a wide-eyed death bat standing there, fur as white as a winter's snow. Luna sipped at a soda before shuffling into the living room and flopping on the couch. A small, round furball sat on the counter, his eyes wide and black.

The queen of the undines sniffed, wiped her eyes and gave Vicky another squeeze. "I'm …"

Zola held up her hand as Vicky joined Luna. "Did you get it?"

"This?" Nixie asked as she fished the Eye of Atlantis out of her pouch.

Zola sagged into the couch, the relief plain to see on the old woman's face.

"Thank the gods," Aideen muttered, leaning over in her chair. "I can't lose anyone else, so help me."

Panic struck at Nixie's heart. "Foster? Is he okay?"

"Oh yes!" Aideen said. "Sorry, I didn't mean to scare you. He's still in Falias. Let me see those scars. What in the world did that to you? It was truly fire demons?"

"I don't know what else they could have been. The Eye was in a cage of sorts in the Abyss. Like it was in its own private plane of existence."

Aideen grimaced. "A barbaric tradition. Long ago, Faerie used to enslave demons to guard their more valuable artifacts. It was a practice abandoned well before the rise of the Mad King."

Nixie rolled the Eye between her fingers.

"Let me take a look at that," Zola said, extending her hand.

Nixie held out the small blue orb.

The old Cajun took it and studied it for a time. "I see where it got its name. If I didn't know better, I could almost think this was an actual Eye."

"It's a weapon, Zola. With enough power to slay a great many water witches. I only hope we can harness its power to help Damian."

Zola nodded. "It should be enough to anchor one of the cores. To transfer it to someone else." Her voice lowered and Nixie almost missed the whisper. "Some-*thing* else."

Aideen launched herself off the coffee table and fluttered to Nixie's shoulder. "Sit down. I need to see your face."

Exhaustion threated to pull Nixie to her knees anyway, so she didn't argue. She sat on a high-backed orange chair and winced when Aideen started poking at the scar tissue.

"Who healed you?" Aideen asked.

"An elderly undine I met in Atlantis," Nixie said. "Shamus. I think he may be a descendant of the line of kings, but he wants nothing to do with ruling the old city."

Aideen leaned back so Nixie could better see her. "A male undine? And, umm, isn't the city dead?"

"Not as dead as we thought. Several deserters moved there when the wars began. And apparently some arrived long before that. And they're living in peace with the blue men of the Minch."

"Well that explains where *they* disappeared to," Aideen said.

"Shamus used some kind of poultice wrapped in kelp and fed me something that tasted like the bottom of Damian's refrigerator."

"Oh gross," Vicky said, revulsion plain on her face.

Aideen barked out a laugh. "That's … graphic. I'm familiar with the concoction, or at least the story of it. It gives some credence to the idea he may be from another age."

The fairy danced on Nixie's shoulder and vanished into her scorched hair. "Okay, so, Shamus did a great job of making you not die, but this is going to hurt like a bitch to fix as Casper would say."

Nixie blew out a breath. "Just get it over with."

"You sure?" Vicky asked. "Dudes dig scars."

Nixie narrowed her eyes at Vicky, and then the pain ignited across her body. Her teeth ground together, and instinct drove her to try to shift to water, escape the pain, but no matter what she did, Aideen kept her trapped in the incantation.

The fairy's face twisted as she moved her hands down Nixie's neck, up behind her ear, and finally traced the savaged flesh around her left eye until it felt she'd burst into flames at any moment.

"Fuck! Me!" Nixie barked when Aideen finally pulled away and the white light of the incantation faded to nothing.

Luna's nose twitched as she slowly raised a handful of cheeseballs to her mouth. The crunch filled the silence of the cabin, an odd contrast to the quiet.

"Ah've seen worse," Zola said.

"That's … *very helpful*," Nixie muttered. She turned her gaze back to Aideen when the fairy tugged at her armor.

"Do you mind?" Aideen asked.

"Mind what?"

Aideen sighed and rolled her eyes before exploding into her full-sized form. An eruption of fairy dust sprayed against the wall.

"My cheeseballs!" Luna yelled, covering the bowl as the cloud of glittering fairy dust settled around them.

Vicky tossed a few back, running her tongue over her teeth. "They're still good. Foster tastes way worse."

Aideen arched an eyebrow, opened her mouth to speak, and instead just muttered to herself. She undid the straps of Nixie's greaves and checked the skin beneath. Pale flesh waited below.

"Perhaps a bit pinker than normal," Aideen said, "but I think you should see a full recovery. I hate to think what might have happened if Shamus hadn't been there."

Nixie flexed her hand and traced the lines of her face that had been scarred. The skin felt smooth again, and only a ghostly hint of pain lingered.

CHAPTER FIFTEEN

VICKY REACHED OUT and took the Eye from Zola. "It doesn't feel like the heart. When I held the Heart of Quindaro, I could almost feel its power, its age. I can't really explain it."

"The Eye of Atlantis has to be unlocked for anyone other than a water witch to use it," Nixie said. "But the key hasn't been seen since the city fell."

Zola hesitated. "And how then do you propose *we* use it?"

Nixie gave her a knowing look. "A gift from a fire demon. Hidden in an old book few people know how to read."

"The Book that Bleeds?" Zola asked. "Even Ah can't read all those pages, girl. What the hell am Ah supposed to do with that?"

"Speak the incantation. I'm sure Damian gave it to you, didn't he? In case something went wrong? In case one day you needed a weapon against the water witches?"

Zola looked away for a moment before returning her gaze to Nixie. "He said to never use that spell because it could kill every one of you."

Nixie inclined her head. "It is dangerous, to be sure. I was somewhat surprised he didn't try to use it against Lewena." She took a deep breath. "What Vicky holds in her hand is the other half."

"But you'll be okay?" Vicky asked. "If we manage to save Damian and he finds out you're dead, I don't think that would go very well."

"If we save Damian and any of us are dead ..." Nixie said, letting the words trail off as a small smile lifted her lips. "I think that would be a very bad day for Gwynn Ap Nudd."

"Let's just make damn sure none of us are dead," Zola snapped. "You saw what happened to him in that battle with Hern. We lost him in earnest. Dragged into the Abyss by Gaia, like some kind of waiting room for his own demise? And if what Terrence said is true, and Ah've little reason to doubt that ghost, and Damian is trapped inside of that thing ... He knows where he is. Frozen, unable to move inside his own body. And is he witnessing the atrocities that his own body has committed?"

"I don't know," Nixie said, her voice barely above a whisper.

"And you remember how torn he was when he worried he might be a dark necromancer like Philip Pinkerton?" Zola rifled through the box, clearly looking for something. "Do you remember how much that tore him in half? Even if we save him now, Ah don't know he'll be the same when he comes out of this."

"It's better than letting him die," Vicky said. "I couldn't live with myself if we just let him go."

Zola took a deep breath. "Me either, girl. Me either." She paused and pulled out a small folded sheet of colorful paper. Translucent blood dripped from it for a moment, and then it was gone. "Hold the book upside down? *Aperio tectus vene—*"

"That's the one," Nixie said as she frowned at Zola. "Did Damian write that incantation down on a brochure?"

Zola's lips twitched. "Looks like it, girl."

Nixie may have been several centuries older than Zola, but something about the old Cajun referring to her as a girl felt more amusing than disrespectful.

"What's next?" Nixie asked. "What do you need from me?"

"You've already done more than any of us could have asked," Vicky said.

"Mmm," Zola said, nodding her head. "Ah agree

with Vicky. You should go home. There's no more you can do for Damian right now. You won't be doing any of us any favors if you lose control of the water witches. Or worse, if you have a fallout with the United Nations."

"Home … it doesn't feel like home without Damian." Nixie studied the back of the gauntlet on her left hand. "It doesn't feel like home without any of you there. Alexandra and Euphemia are like sisters to me, but there is still an emptiness that I can't explain. Some of that felt filled in Atlantis. I don't know if that makes any sense."

Zola reached forward and patted Nixie's knee. "Ah think you've explained it just fine. Sometimes family is more than what you have by blood or marriage. And it would do us all well to remember that. It will get you through the darker times."

"Zola did talk to Koda," Vicky said.

"Don't remind me," Zola muttered. "That damn ghost will be the death of me."

"Did you learn more about gifting Gaia's powers to Damian?" Nixie asked, leaning forward.

Zola pursed her lips and picked up a dark green crystal, not unlike a shard of quartz, but shot through with flecks and streaks the color of blood.

"Is that a bloodstone?" Luna asked, licking orange

cheese dust off her fingertips.

"Tessrian's bloodstone," Zola said. "And Ah'm afraid we're not getting around talking to that old demon again."

"The Burning Lands?" Nixie asked.

Zola inclined her head. "Koda believes at least one of the artifacts Gaia needs is in a vault beyond the Sea of Souls. So Ah guess Ah'm stuck asking that damned parrot for help."

Nixie wasn't sure if Zola was more irritated with the idea of going to the Burning Lands, or of having to go there with Graybeard. Either way, she fought back a smile.

The old Cajun sighed and reached into the chest at the base of the coffee table again. "Might as well get this over with."

"Oh, that's gross," Luna said, still not breaking her rhythm as she stuffed another handful of cheeseballs in her face.

Zola grimaced as the Book that Bleeds poured translucent blood across her hands. It pooled on the coffee table and dripped to the floor, only to vanish an instant before it hit.

"Is this safe to use in the presence of the children?" Aideen asked.

Vicky cocked an eyebrow and Luna finally stopped

crunching on cheeseballs.

"Ah, yes, I mean the young adults?"

"Better," Vicky said.

Luna narrowed her wide eyes and swiveled her ears back and forth. "I forgive you."

"We'll know soon enough." Zola turned the Book that Bleeds upside down and spoke the incantation, "*Aperio tectus veneficium!*"

The book writhed in her hands, and Nixie cringed at the smoke and ear-piercing whine that rose from the bloody book. A sliver of silver slipped from the binding, red hot as it crashed down and sizzled against the coffee table. The book stopped moving, and Zola slid it back into the trunk with a shiver.

"Ah don't like that thing. Not one bit."

Thunder crashed above them before a sickly orange light from outside turned the entire room a grotesque shade of pumpkin. Nixie's hand slid to the dagger sheathed at her ankle.

Vicky lit a soulsword.

Aideen stalked to the door.

Luna set down her cheeseballs.

Something roared as shadows and flame lashed out from behind the old oak tree. Nixie cursed and lunged ahead of Aideen.

The broad blackened horns of a fire demon swung

side to side in the early sunset. Nixie's heart stuttered in her chest until she recognized the symmetrical teeth and angled snout. As she watched, the horns curled in on themselves and healthy flesh slid up the legs of the demon, discoloring until a leather apron materialized around a barrel-chested torso. When it was done, Mike the Demon stood before her, hammer at the ready, and relief on his face.

"No fight then?" a smaller woman asked as she stepped out from behind Mike. Sarah, the little necromancer, someone who knew how to get into some serious shit when they were still alive was how Damian had put it.

"Nudd's balls," Aideen muttered, snapping into her smaller form and flopping onto Zola's shoulder as she slid past Nixie.

Jasper peeked out from under the coffee table, looked around the room, and then retreated back into the shadows.

"What the hell are you doing here?" Zola asked, reaching out to Mike for a hug as they met at the bottom of the stairs to the porch. "And where the fuck have you been?"

"Someone unlocked the Book that Bleeds," Mike said, wrapping her up in muscled arms. "I was worried it might not be one of us."

And there it was. Just those words calmed the unsettled fear in Nixie's gut. Mike was still their friend. Those demons in the Abyss were something else, something darker, and nothing like her friend and ally.

"Sarah and I have been in and out of the Burning Lands. It's been left in upheaval since Prosperine was slain." He glanced up at Vicky as he released Zola.

Vicky rolled her eyes. "You can say Prosperine out loud. I won't have a seizure."

Zola nodded slowly. "We may need to discuss the Burning Lands a bit more. An odd place for a honeymoon, though."

"Does this mean you got the Eye?" Sarah asked. "You're really going to try to re-anchor a blood knot? I wish I could see that. Now *that* would be a honeymoon. You all are crazy. My kind of people."

Mike pinched the bridge of his nose and sighed.

"Better crazy than dead," Vicky muttered, punching Mike in the arm. "Hey!" she squawked as Mike picked her up into a bone-crushing hug of her own.

"My god, you look old," Sarah said.

Vicky looked down at herself and frowned.

"No, I just mean we must be getting old. *So old.*"

Mike smacked his lips and ignored the next full minute of Sarah explaining just how *old* he was. "As to the question? You have the Eye of Atlantis?"

"Luna could you—" Zola started.

The death bat zipped inside, shouted something about a fire, and then reappeared. "Fire's out. Coffee table is a little, uh, scorched." She flicked her thumb and sent a small blue orb spiraling through the air.

Nixie caught it at the bottom of the short stairs and held it up to Mike.

"You have the tools now," Mike said. "You must unlock the Eye if you mean to use it."

"What about you?" Nixie asked. "Is this going to kill you? Your oath?"

Mike shrugged. The most infuriatingly vague response he could have possibly come up with. "It shouldn't. As long as you don't use the Eye to turn all of your undines to stone?"

"I think I can resist."

CHAPTER SIXTEEN

THEY GATHERED BEHIND the cabin, taking up random seats around the ring of stone Aeros had raised so long ago. Zola studied the silver metal with the incantation on it.

"I thought you said this would be a fallen art." She raised her eyes to Mike.

"I assume it fell out of the book?" the fire demon said with a straight face.

Zola groaned. "You did not just say that. This is Fae magic."

"It's older than that," Mike said.

Aideen paced back and forth on Zola's shoulder. "I'm going to be very upset if we blow up."

Mike held his palms out. "I promise no one will explode." And, as an afterthought, he added, "Today."

Zola sighed and held up the Eye of Atlantis. "What the hell else are we going to do?" Without further warning, she spoke. "*Omnia Caritas Destuit!*"

The Eye cracked in her hand, tiny fissures racing

around the surface until the shell collapsed, and a brilliant ball of blue energy remained. It still looked like the Eye of Atlantis, but where before it had appeared more like a marble, it now seemed more like a tiny blue sun.

"It's beautiful," Sarah said.

Wisps of pale magic lifted from the edge of the Eye and swirled about it like a hurricane, only to settle once more onto the blue surface.

"Two cores," Zola said. "All we need now is the third."

"And an anchor," Nixie said. "Gaia said we'll need an anchor for the blood knot."

Zola nodded. "Ah know, girl."

"Gaia said …" Nixie trailed off. "Gaia said Damian is fading. We only have a few days at most." She didn't miss the shiver that ran down Vicky's spine.

Aideen cursed.

"Buck up," Zola said. "That just means we have to hurry." She frowned at the Eye of Atlantis. "And perhaps split our focus up more than Ah'd hoped. Ah doubt Nudd will sit idly by."

Nixie nodded. "Considering what attacked Puerto Rico today, he's already done being idle."

"What happened in Puerto Rico?" Mike asked.

Luna started tapping on her phone, her claws still

clicking across the screen as she used the pads of her fingers. "Here."

Nixie could hear the newscast start up as Mike and Sarah watched in ever-increasing shock.

"Ah'll speak with Koda and Happy," Zola said. "They're in contact with the Society of Flame about some other potential anchors. They need to know our timeframe just closed up on us."

"We can help," Vicky said.

"I'll do anything for a can of cheeseballs," Luna said as she almost purred.

Vicky raised an eyebrow. "You're going to end up with high blood pressure by the time we get you back to Camazotz."

"Foster needs to know what's happening," Aideen said. "I'll return to Falias. Morrigan should know, too. Heavens knows what's coming."

Nixie reached out to Zola who handed her the Eye of Atlantis. It brightened at the touch of the water witch and the fresh scent of the sea washed over the clearing. She took a deep breath before handing it back to Zola, and the smells of the firepit were all that remained.

"I entrust this to you. It is our most sacred artifact, one never meant to leave Atlantis. Whatever you need to do to save Vicky, do it."

She met Zola's gaze, and the deep brown of the woman's eyes promised everything they didn't say aloud.

Zola slipped the Eye of Atlantis into a pocket inside her cloak, where the blue light vanished entirely.

"Since you're here," Zola said, tugging on Mike's arm. "Why don't we talk about vacationing in the Burning Lands."

"You're going to drag them into this now?" Aideen asked from her perch on Zola's shoulder.

"Drag them in?" Zola asked. "They've already been there. And recently!"

"We have no idea what they might have planned. What if they're planning something else to help Damian?"

"Nonsense. They aren't Sunday Soldiers. Ah'm sure they'd march right back into the Burning Lands to help Damian."

"Ooo, sounds fun!" Sarah said, following the pair.

Mike tripped up the stairs after Zola. "Wait, what?"

Nixie turned back to Vicky and Luna. "You two keep an eye on them."

Luna nodded.

"Sure," Vicky said. "And you try not to break up the United Nations and sink the world into chaos, yeah?"

Nixie blinked and gave Vicky a slow smile. "I'll do what I can."

"You leaving now?" Luna asked. "We have a pond. Do you sleep in ponds? I don't know much about water witches."

Nixie grinned at the death bat. "I have to go, Luna. But watch over our friends, will you? We'll meet again soon." She waved to Vicky and Luna before running her fingers across the back of the gauntlet and stepping into the Abyss.

CHAPTER SEVENTEEN

NUDD STOOD IN darkness. There were few things that could unsettle the old king, but being at the mercy of an Unseelie Fae's magic was certainly one of those. There were some incantations that the Unseelie had mastered, magicks that Seelie Fae, and even those who lay somewhere in between, could not use effectively.

So instead, Nudd waited in shadow. The nauseating swirl of the Warded Ways would have been a welcome sight in that place. Instead, there was only silence and darkness, until something in the shadows breathed.

"Your gambit has failed in Atlantis," a voice said.

"My Lord," Nudd said. "It is not a failure, only a delay. The undine retrieved the Eye of Atlantis. It is exposed, almost within our grasp."

"You were given instructions that should you summon one of the crawling chaos, you would unleash it upon the world in full. Confining it to that flesh crippled it, and led to the death of a creature of infinite age."

"Once the weapon is retrieved from the Abyss—"

"Your weapon is lost. Your promise nearly broken. Open the gateway between worlds and let us through, or the dark touched vampires at your side will become the least of your worries."

"Of course, my Lord. The incantation is nearly complete. Once the construction of the gate has been finished, you will be welcomed into this world."

The voice in the darkness growled. "See that it is so, Gwynn Ap Nudd. Our Unseelie allies warned us that you were deceptive, and our patience is not infinite. See this done."

Nudd tried to respond but no sound would come, as if the very air had been ripped from his lungs as his body was pulled back through the Unseelie gateway. He slammed onto the stone floor of his throne room, monolithic columns sweeping up beside him, and two chanting Fae standing to either side.

"Welcome back."

Nudd struggled to his feet and made his way back up to the throne. He took two deep breaths, steadying himself, unwilling to show any crack in his façade to the Unseelie Fae. The eldritch gods thought it was Nudd who had failed to retrieve the Eye. But his plan had gone perfectly; it was the Unseelie Fae who failed.

They'd failed to penetrate Atlantis, failed to steal the Eye at the surface, and only one of them had even managed to survive. The eldritch gods promised Nudd an army to march behind his weapon. But the dark touched and the Unseelie Fae had failed again and again. Even if he succeeded, Nudd wondered if it was time to seek help elsewhere. If the time for old alliances had come and gone, or if the seals should be thrown wide, and the ancient gods of destruction loosed upon the earth once more.

Note from Eric R. Asher

Thank you for spending time with the misfits! I'm blown away by the fantastic reader response to this series, and am so grateful to you all. The next book of misadventures is called *The Book of the Staff*, and it's available soon (or maybe now because I'm lazy about updating these things).

If you'd like an email when each new book releases, sign up for my mailing list (www.ericrasher.com). Emails only go out about once per month and your information is closely guarded by hungry cu siths.

Also, follow me on BookBub (bookbub.com/authors/eric-r-asher), and you'll always get an email for special sales.

Thanks for reading!
Eric

The Book of the Staff
The Vesik Series, book #12
By Eric R. Asher

Also by Eric R. Asher

Keep track of Eric's new releases by receiving an email on release day. It's fast and easy to sign up for Eric's mailing list, and you'll also get an ebook copy of the subscriber exclusive anthology, *Whispers of War*.

Go here to get started: www.ericrasher.com

The Steamborn Trilogy:

Steamborn
Steamforged
Steamsworn

The Vesik Series:

(Recommended for Ages 17+)

Days Gone Bad
Wolves and the River of Stone
Winter's Demon
This Broken World
Destroyer Rising
Rattle the Bones
Witch Queen's War
Forgotten Ghosts
The Book of the Ghost
The Book of the Claw
The Book of the Sea

The Book of the Staff*
The Book of the Rune*
The Book of the Sails*
The Book of the Wing*
The Book of the Blade*
The Book of the Fang*
The Book of the Reaper*

The Vesik Series Box Sets

Box Set One (Books 1-3)
Box Set Two (Books 4-6)
Box Set Three (Books 7-8)
Box Set Four: The Books of the Dead Part 1
(Coming in 2020)*
Box Set Five: The Books of the Dead Part 2
(Coming in 2020)*

Mason Dixon – Monster Hunter:

Episode One
Episode Two
Episode Three

*Want to receive an email when one of Eric's books
releases? Sign up for Eric's mailing list.
www.ericrasher.com

About the Author

Eric is a former bookseller, cellist, and comic seller currently living in Saint Louis, Missouri. A lifelong enthusiast of books, music, toys, and games, he discovered a love for the written word after being dragged to the library by his parents at a young age. When he is not writing, you can usually find him reading, gaming, or buried beneath a small avalanche of Transformers. For more about Eric, see: www.ericrasher.com

Enjoy this book? You can make a big difference.

Reviews are the most powerful tools I have when it comes to getting attention for my books. I don't have a huge marketing budget like some New York publishers, but I have something even better.

A committed and loyal bunch of readers.

Honest reviews help bring my books to the attention of other readers.

If you've enjoyed this book, I would be very grateful if you could take a minute to leave a review. It can be as short as you like. Thank you for spending time with Damian and the misfits.

Connect with Eric R. Asher Online:

Twitter: @ericrasher

Instagram: @ericrasher

Facebook: EricRAsher

www.ericrasher.com

eric@ericrasher.com

Made in the USA
Monee, IL
27 March 2023

30622348R00094